"Hugh Ashton's new book is ready to come out, and it's a doozy. I predict a Hollywood blockbuster to follow."

"Mr. Ashton has created a sympathetic anti-hero, and provided him with a world to inhabit that is both frightening and tragic. A chilling and intense thriller."

"A fantastic read. Heartbreaking to know the realism is mirror to life and families really do lose their homes in such a fashion."

"Henry Powers is the new Bronsonsque vigilante who takes on the Wall Street criminals who dumped fraudulent mortgages, and were given a free pass in our two-tiered justice system. I have to admit that I ended up rooting for Powers and didn't shed a tear for the arrogant Wall Street types that he shot."

Balance of Powers

Hugh Ashton

ISBN-10: 1-91-260561-9
ISBN-13: 978-1-912605-61-3
Published by j-views Publishing, 2019

© 2015, 2019 Hugh Ashton and j-views Publishing

All rights reserved. Without limiting the rights under copyright reserved above, no part of this publication may be reproduced, stored in or introduced into a retrieval system, or transmitted, in any form, or by any means (electronic, mechanical, photocopying, recording, or otherwise) without the prior written permission of both the copyright owner and the above publisher of this book.
This is a work of fiction. Names, characters, places, brands, media, and incidents are either the product of the author's imagination or are written in respectful tribute to the originals.

www.HughAshtonBooks.com
www.j-views.biz

j-views Publishing, 26 Lombard Street, Lichfield, WS13 6DR UK

BALANCE OF POWERS

THIS BOOK is dedicated to those who have suffered as a result of actions similar to those described in this book, in the sincere hope that change will come that makes it impossible for such things to happen in the future.

ACKNOWLEDGEMENTS AND THANKS

As ALWAYS, a book is more than just one person's work. As I wrote this book, I was conscious of all the influences on me, and all the help I have received.

This book has been an emotional roller-coaster for me, as I write outside my comfort zone, and I thank my wife, Yoshiko, for her constant support.

To all my Facebook friends living in the USA, including those who kindly read through parts of the story, and helped me with some of the characterization and the localization of the story.

Special thanks to Perry Constantine, who educated me in the fine art of pulp fiction cover design.

More thanks to Andy Boerger, who suggested amplifications and changes to critical parts of the story, resulting in a better book at the end of the day.

Many thanks to Bev Thomas, who generously provided the practical advice at the end of this book, addressed to all who may have suffered at the hands of the predatory lenders.

And heartfelt thanks to the Inknbeans Press staff and the other Inknbeans authors for their support and encouragement when the original edition of this book was published.

BALANCE OF POWERS

HUGH ASHTON

J-VIEWS PUBLISHING, LICHFIELD, UK

KENDRA HAMPTON STOOD WAITING on the Manhattan street, watching people entering the office building. The wind blew off the water along the almost deserted roadway. She shivered, and it wasn't just because of the cold. This wasn't her thing at all. She should have called the cops, and let them deal with the situation. It wasn't her job to go in as Wonder Woman and save the world.

A little worm of fear was eating its way through her insides. It wasn't the simple fear of failure that sometimes overcame her when she was given a task that seemed too hard, though God knows this wasn't going to be easy. It was a far more elemental fear – the fear of dying.

Or was it even that simple? she asked herself. Perhaps not so much being frightened of dying as being terrified of meeting a primeval uncontrollable force. What she'd been told made her believe once again in demons. She'd stopped going to church when she went to college, but a part of her still remembered the devils and angels of her childhood. Hell had always seemed more real than Heaven to her, and the demons closer to us than angels.

And now, if what she had been told was correct, she was about to meet a demon, face to face.

A passerby, seemingly oblivious of anything except the latte he was drinking from a travel mug, bumped into her, and swore reflexively before offering a brief insincere apology. It shook her out of her thoughts. There are no such things as demons, her rational side told the other side of herself. You are here to meet a man, not some supernatural fairy tale monster.

She looked around, to see if she could see her quarry. He shouldn't be hard to spot, even in a crowd. On this almost empty street, there was no way she could miss him. A small crowd of people spilled out of an office building nearby, not the one she was watching, and she scanned them to see if he was with them.

And then the enormity of the task before her hit, and the worm started crawling once more. A powerful man, physically and mentally, driven by revenge to desperate acts, and about to carry out the most desperate so far, unless she could stop him. She, Kendra Hampton, was the only thing that stood between the deaths of perhaps dozens of people and their safety. She shivered again.

MAJOR HENRY GILLETTE POWERS straightened his cap, taking one last look at himself in the mirror. Gotta look smart – Marine smart – he told himself. Go out of the Corps on your last day looking better than you went in. He smiled to himself, thinking of the wet rag of a shavetail he'd been less than ten years before.

Well, not that much of a wet rag, he guessed, or the Corps would never have taken him on. But Parris Island, Quantico, and the tours in Afghanistan had definitely toughened him and brought him to the point where he could walk tall and unafraid through the meanest streets, and know that no-one was going to dare lay a finger on him. Major Powers, in or out of uniform, was not someone that you wanted to mess with. And it wasn't the street-style, gang-member kind of tough that he exuded. No sir, Major Powers was six foot three of the kind of muscle and sinew that no gym could ever give you, and carried with a pride in what he was and what he had fought for.

He'd done his share of killing, but that wasn't what he was proudest of. Unlike some of his fellow Marines, he'd never taken pleasure in finding a man in his sights and squeezing the trigger. The man who fell to the ground after the bullet hit him was a mother's son. Maybe she still loved him, maybe she didn't. Maybe he had a wife and children. Powers was always aware that he was taking the life of another human being – a human being, admittedly, who would kill him if not killed first – but still a node in the complex web of humanity.

His Navy Cross had been won as a lieutenant, not for taking life, but for saving it. His platoon had been pinned down by a group of Afghan resistance fighters in the mountains to the south of Kabul. One of the platoon had an arm shattered by an AK-47 bullet, and another had suddenly developed abdominal pains which Lieutenant Powers strongly suspected were a symptom of acute appendicitis. There was no way out of the gully in which they were sheltering without exposing the Marine platoon to a withering fire from the Afghans. Their radio had taken a hit from a stray bullet, and they were unable to call for help. None of the air patrols seemed to have spotted them, and the situation seemed hopeless.

Willis, the Marine with suspected appendicitis, moaned uncontrollably as the pain struck once more, and the young officer made up his mind. He tied a white flag to the end of his carbine, and waved it above the gully. Good, no shots were directed at it. His heart in his mouth, he slowly stood up, raising his hands in the air, exposing his head and shoulders to the Taliban not two hundred yards away.

"You surrender, Yankee?" came a shout in accented English.

"No!" he yelled back. "I want to talk."

"Come here and talk," was the reply.

Ignoring the mutters from his men of "the looie's gone crazy" and "what the fuck does he think he's doing?", he climbed out of the gully, and, hands held high, made his way towards the Taliban.

When he was about ten yards away from the nearest of them, the harsh voice that had spoken earlier commanded him to stop. The speaker was still invisible.

"What do you want?" it asked.

"One of my men is sick. He needs a doctor. I want your promise that if two more of my men help him to make his way to a doctor, none of them will be harmed by you." He had no idea if his words were understood. There was silence, broken only by the buzzing of a fly around his head, settling on his face, drinking the sweat, and then taking off for another orbit, but he kept his hands high, fearing that any sudden move would be misinterpreted.

At length, the voice said, "What sort of sick is your man?"

Moving as slowly as he could, Lieutenant Powers pointed to his side. "Bad pain here."

"One of our men, too," said the voice. "Can your doctor make this pain go away?"

"If he sees my man soon, yes. If not, my man will die."

There was a burst of talking in Pashtun, of which the American officer understood not a word. Then, "Do you Yankee doctors help anyone?"

Powers remembered what he knew of the Hippocratic oath. "Yes."

"You would help my son?"

Powers thought quickly. It seemed he was talking to one of the leaders of the band. Who knew what a little kindness would bring? "Yes, we will help."

"You take him to your doctor?"

"Yes. If you will let my sick man and his helpers go free."

"We let you all go free if you help my Shaheed. Now go back to your men, Yankee. Come back with two of them. Shaheed will be waiting for them to carry him."

Half-fearing a bullet in the back, Powers turned slowly and returned to his men. "Jabonski, Petersen, we have a sick man out there who needs the medics. Come with me and bring him in."

"Excuse me, sir, but we're all here. I don't think

anyone's sick except Willis and he's here with us."

"He's not one of our platoon, Jabonski. He's one of them. Drop your weapons and move!"

"Sir? What if it's a trap?"

"Then we're dead, aren't we?" The two Marines appeared to hesitate. "That was an order, Petersen. You remember what an order is? Follow me."

"Yes sir." They followed Powers across the stony wasteland.

"Here he is," said Powers, as they came to the skinny Afghan boy, seemingly no more than twelve years old, moaning in pain. "Poor kid."

"He's just a raghead," said Pedersen. "Better we just leave him. One camel jockey less for us to deal with."

"One more crack like that, Corporal, and you'll be busted down to private so fast you won't know what's hit you. Now pick him up, you two, and carry him – as gently as if he was your own son."

"Why are we doing this, sir?" asked Jabonski as they made their way back to their own position.

"Because I have just promised to help this kid."

"And what do we get out of it, then, sir?" The tone was just short of insolent.

"Our lives," said Powers. "I've been promised that we can all walk away if we get this boy to a doctor."

Despite the Marines' skepticism, as they left the gully in which they had taken cover, led by Powers, no shots rang out. Instead, the voice came from over the plain. "The blessings of Allah upon you, Yankee."

"And may His blessings rest on you, my friend!" Powers shouted back.

When the platoon reached the base, the doctors worked on both Willis and the Afghan boy Shaheed, and they made a full recovery. Lieutenant Powers made a full report of the incident, and was commended for his resourcefulness and his skill in extraditing his platoon from a potentially disastrous situation.

It wasn't the end of the story, though. About two weeks after the incident in the gully, a group of unarmed tribesmen were admitted to the Marine camp, where they asked to see Shaheed, describing him as "my son who the tall black Yankee saved from death".

Powers was out on patrol when they called, but after visiting Shaheed in the field hospital, the leader demanded to see the Marine officer in command, to whom he pledged that his band would no longer fight against the invaders. "For we know," he explained, "that there is at least one good man among you. Maybe more. Let us try peace rather than war."

The Marine colonel somewhat bemusedly shook hands with the chieftain to seal the agreement, and to everyone's surprise, peace suddenly broke out over the area.

"I don't know quite how you managed it, Lieutenant, but you did it. I'm putting you forward for Captain, and recommending you for the Navy Cross. I don't know how many lives you've saved, but you've made my job a hell of a sight easier. Good work."

JUST ANOTHER DAY at the office, Kendra Hampton sighed to herself, looking round the room. Almost as far as the eye could see, the screens on every desk flickered and spat out the raw information that the New York newsroom processed and delivered to the subscribers of the service all over the world. The news coming in – an incipient Middle Eastern war, a gridlock in the US Senate, a Eurozone crisis, seemed about par for the course, and hardly merited a headline on the Website of this massive multinational news organization.

Kendra Hampton's particular speciality was a small corner of the financial services sector, namely the complex bond derivatives that the Wall Street firms traded in vast profitable quantities. She'd started her working life as an analyst in Bear Stearns, and later moving to a more senior position, but still as a grunt, in Lehman Brothers, sensing that there was something strange in the way that Bear was going.

It didn't take her long at Lehman before the same feeling appeared again. It seemed to her that the whole of Wall Street was a house of cards, waiting for just a little nudge before the whole edifice came tumbling to the ground. She talked to some of her friends in other firms, giving away as little about what she personally felt about the situation at Lehman, and realized that her misgivings were not hers alone, nor was the general malaise restricted to the firms where she had been working. Time to get out, she told herself.

Her knowledge and expertise immediately landed her a job with one of the financial magazines, where, within a month of working there, her analysis of the bond markets won her an industry award, and a new job offer from her current employer, Financial News Services, usually abbreviated to FNS.

The hours were long, and the work was hard, but the pay was good. In any case, Hampton was used to the long hours of hard work from her time in the investment banks, and she enjoyed the pressure of deadlines. She was considered to be one of the best in the business at what she did, and her work was read around the world by a small, but highly select, group of financial professionals who valued her analysis. In return for her advice, a small stable of traders kept her well supplied with knowledge and views from inside the industry, and quotes when needed.

Right now, she wanted one of those quotes to liven up the article she was writing – something colorful and pithy. Charlie Sanfion was always good for a quote. The usual obscene reference, after Hampton had sanitized it a little, made for good copy, and usually hooked readers into the rest of the article.

She picked up the phone and hit the speed dial button that would connect her to Sanfion's desk. After three rings, there was still no answer – most unlike Charlie. Either he pounced on the phone and mashed the line key as soon as the light flashed on his dealer "turret", as the complex trader phone systems were known, or he forwarded the call to another station if he was going to be away from his desk for more than ten seconds.

Hampton checked her calendar. It wasn't a public holiday or anything. It was easy to forget these things, working where she did, where news from round the world was a 24/7 event, and time and date faded into irrelevance.

Ah well, she'd have to try another of her pets if Charlie wasn't going to pick up the phone. She hit another speed dial key, and got the alternate pet's quote. Not as good as Charlie would have provided, for sure, and it didn't really say what she wanted. Damn, back to Charlie.

This time the phone was picked up on the second ring.

"Yes?" The voice wasn't Charlie's.

"Hi there, it's Kendra Hampton from FNS," she

identified herself. "Charlie's not at his desk? Is he around?"

There was a pause of several seconds before the answer came back. "Charlie's not— Let me just say that Charlie's not working here any more."

Hampton felt stunned. Charles Sanfion had been working for over twenty years at that firm. "Has he, er, been let go?"

"Not really. Look, I can't talk to you about this. If you want to know about Charlie, you'll have to talk to Corporate Communications, OK? Gotta hop." And the line went dead.

As it happened, Hampton did want to know what had happened to Charlie Sanfion. Though it would be a stretch to call him a friend, over the time she'd been working at FNS, they'd developed a good personal relationship. Added to which, it was going to be hard to find another source of the sarcastic obscene wit that marked Sanfion's pronouncements on the bond market.

Though she held out little hope, she called Corporate Communications at Sanfion's firm and explained what she wanted.

"It's not our policy to talk about personal matters concerning our employees," she heard.

"So it's a personal issue?"

"I am not allowed to tell you whether it's personal or not. All I can say to you at this time is that Charles Sanfion is no longer working here."

"Can you tell me where he is working now?" Hampton persisted.

"I am not authorized to give you that

information."

Well, she hadn't really expected anything more from these people. She'd tried and failed in the past when she wanted information from them, and knew that compared to them, the Mafia code of omertà was the verbal equivalent of diarrhea.

Well, there were other ways of finding out. She could make her way to one of the cigar bars where the traders and salesmen from Charlie's floor usually hung out and keep her ears open. She liked the smell of cigar smoke, and had been known to smoke a cigar herself from time to time, somewhat to the bemusement of the Wall Street traders who used the place as their watering hole. She knew some of them well enough that they would talk off the record to her on occasion. But all this wasn't getting the article written, and she had a deadline to meet. Damn it, it was worrying if Charlie Sanfion had suddenly disappeared off the face of the earth. It nagged at her mind all through the day, and she decided that he was going to find out what had happened, if at all possible.

HER PARTNER, LIZ, was used to her "Working late. Be with you soon. Love you." texts like the one she sent off as she made her way to the bar where she ordered a drink and waited for the traders to appear.

A group of traders whom she recognized as coming from Charlie's floor made their way into the bar. Usually these people were noisy and exuberant, but this evening they were quiet and subdued. If she hadn't seen the figures just before she left the office, Hampton would have sworn that the markets had taken a dive. Mind you, up or down, the investment banks still made money. Maybe one of them had made a disastrous trade.

She strained to hear their conversation over the sound of the commentary of the Yankees game on the big-screen TV, but could only hear "To Charlie," as they raised their glasses in what appeared to be a solemn toast.

"He was the best," she heard one of them say

during a lull in the ballgame commentary.

"There'll never be another like him," another agreed, downing his drink as the batter hit a double RBI, and the commentator went wild, drowning out any replies.

So Charlie Sanfion was history? Well, she'd worked that out, hadn't she, but what sort of history were they talking about? Had he really died? It seemed like it from the way they were talking and acting.

The traders standing at the bar went into a huddle, standing very close together, and their voices went very quiet. Even when there was silence from the TV screen, it was impossible for Hampton to hear what they were saying.

She recognized one of them, Tommy, who seemed to have been as close to Charles Sanfion as any of them. Tommy caught her eye, turned to speak with one of the other traders, and then made his way over, glass in hand, to the table where Hampton was sitting.

"Go ahead," said Hampton, in answer to the unspoken request to sit at the table.

"It was me you spoke to earlier today when you called Charlie," said Tommy. "Don't know if you recognized my voice or not."

"No, sorry."

"I was told to direct any queries to Corporate Communications. I take it they didn't tell you anything?"

"Of course not. But I had to try, didn't I?"

Tommy took a pull at his drink, emptying the

glass, and from the look on his face, was obviously making up his mind about something. He leaned forward and spoke in a hoarse whisper.

"If I tell you something about Charlie, you must never, ever, let anyone know where you heard it. Okay?"

"Okay."

"First off, Charlie's dead."

So it was what she had suspected. "I'm sorry to hear that. I liked the guy. He may have been crude and rude, but he was a good guy."

Tommy nodded. "Yes, he was."

"Another drink?" Hampton pointed to Tommy's empty glass. You don't mind me buying you a drink?" She smiled, hopefully not too flirtatiously, and with what she hoped was some sympathy. Hampton had the gift of listening, and not forcing the conversation into a particular groove, preferring to guide it gently towards the direction she wanted. For now, she'd wait a moment until Tommy felt ready to talk.

"Sure."

The drinks arrived. Neither said anything until both had raised their glasses in a silent toast to the absent Charlie.

Hampton broke the silence. "Can you tell me more? I'm guessing from everyone's reaction that it wasn't a natural death."

"I'll tell you." He took a long pull at his drink. "I was on the floor. My desk's next to Charlie's, and he wasn't in. No note, no voicemail. Nothing. Had no idea where he was. Someone asked me, and we made some crack about his woman — you know, Carly, the supermodel?"

She nodded.

"The one he bought a house for in the Bahamas to match the one he bought for his wife in St. Nevis or wherever it was. We made some crack about him and her in the back seat of one of his cars. He'd be coming when he was ready. Something pretty tasteless, anyway."

She half-smiled. She knew about traders' sense of humor from her time in the banks. "And then?"

"Jim, over there." He pointed. "He's the head of fixed-income, and he came over and tapped me on the shoulder right in the middle of me talking to a client. You never do that. Never. And I swung round and I was about to pop him one, when I saw his face. You've heard someone say someone else's face was ashen?"

"Yes."

"Well, Jim's face was gray. He looked like he'd seen a ghost. And then he told me that the police had just called him, and told him about Charlie."

"What had they told him?"

"They said he'd been found dead in his car. His Ferrari convertible."

"'Found dead'? Sounds like it wasn't an accident."

"Unless two .45 bullets to the head is an accident, no, it wasn't."

The news shocked her. "Oh, the poor guy. So sorry to hear that. A robbery? Not a carjacking, obviously, if he was still in the car."

"Not according to what I heard the police are saying. This is totally fucking bizarre. Apparently there were three ten-dollar bills stuffed into Charlie's mouth. His billfold wasn't touched. The car keys were still in the ignition. Nothing seemed to be missing."

"He was shot?" Hampton still couldn't really get her head round the idea.

"Twice. In the head. Jim told me that the police say it looks like a professional-style execution with a .45, but they won't know for sure until they've done an autopsy and some ballistics checks."

"Is the Mob mixed up in this, do you think?"

"You know, that's one of the first questions that Jim asked me about Charlie. Did I think he was connected with the Mob? The firm's worried that if he was, and the word gets out, the name of the firm is in the shit." Tommy shook his head. "Typical. The guy gets whacked, and the first thing the firm thinks about its its good name."

"Well?" Hampton raised her eyebrows.

Tommy shook his head. "No way did Charlie ever mention the wiseguys. I can't believe he would get mixed up in anything like that. You probably didn't know Charlie like we did. Came along to Atlantic City with us on our nights out, but never sat at the tables. He always said he got enough excitement trading. Never did blow. Never went with the hookers. Damn it, why would he bother? Maureen, his wife, and Carly on the side. Two gorgeous women. No need to go anywhere else for fun when you had those two ready and waiting."

"Money? Doesn't sound like it if they're leaving money in his mouth. That's really weird, I agree."

Tommy shook his head again. "Charlie got these fucking humongous bonuses, didn't he? He wouldn't need to borrow any money off anyone."

"Those antique cars he collected cost him a fortune."

"Charlie made fucking fortunes. Many times over. He could afford what he did."

"So who would have killed him, and why?"

"I can't think of any reason why anyone would want to kill him. Christ, he was no fucking saint, but he wasn't that bad a guy. And he was one hell of a trader. The biggest swinging dick in the business. He probably made more money for the firm single-handed than the rest of Wall Street put together. And we talk on the Street about going for the kill and playing rough, but we don't mean it that literally."

One of the traders at the bar called over to them. "Tommy, you okay? She giving you a hard time?" He laughed, but it was subdued compared to the usual raucous exuberance of the bond trading floor.

"I'm fine," Tommy called back. He didn't look fine, Hampton thought. He was sweating, though the bar was pleasantly cool, and a muscle under one eye kept twitching. He turned back to Hampton. "Now do you want the really scary part of all this?"

"This isn't scary?"

"It's scary enough. But wait for this. Charlie isn't the first. Just over a week ago, that Swiss bank over the way from us lost their best trader in asset-backeds."

"Lost? How on earth do you lose a trader?"

"Same way as we lost Charlie, Jim told me. The guy was found dead in his car. Two shots to the head with a .45, and three ten-dollar bills stuffed in his mouth."

"Dear sweet Lord. How did Jim know about all this?"

"The police told him. Thought he should know."

"Sounds like it's not a great time to be a fixed-income trader in derivatives. Open season on them. Sorry," she added as Tommy winced visibly. "That was in poor taste, and I apologize."

"Accepted. But you're fucking right there. It does seem like open season on us. All of us are shit scared, I don't mind admitting to you."

"Why are you telling me all this, anyway?"

"You knew Charlie, and he respected you, I know. He told us you were the only guy writing about the business who wasn't talking out his ass. That's one reason."

"I'll take it as a compliment that you called me a guy just then. There's another reason?"

"Yeah. The guys on the floor reckon that if this gets made public, the one who's pulling this shit will get so spooked he'll stop doing it."

"So you want me to write this up as a story? Mentioning Charlie by name, and the Swiss crowd as well?"

Tommy nodded. "That's about the size of it."

"Look, I'm no crime reporter. I'd have to check with the police and so on. I wouldn't know where to start on this one."

"Just tell the story. Just the facts, like I told them to you just now."

"And your management's going to really freak out when they read the story. First thing they're going to ask is, where the heck did this gal get all this from? Who told her all of this?"

"You'd protect your sources, wouldn't you?"

"Sure I would. But you wouldn't have to be the hero of a detective show to work out that it could only have come from one or two places, and the finger's going to start pointing, Tommy. And sooner rather than later it's going to point at you. And then what?"

"We all of us took a vote on whether to tell you. They can't fire the whole floor."

"They could if they felt like it. You know I worked on the Street. Bear and then Lehman. I've seen whole divisions blown up, not just one part of a trading floor, simply because management didn't like the way the head of trading said good morning to the directors. None of you is safe."

"Well, we're not fucking safe with a madman running round putting bullets into people's heads and stuffing their mouths with money. What the hell's the big idea there, anyway?"

"Sounds symbolic, doesn't it? One way of

saying that you're greedy bastards, perhaps?"

"It's a hell of a way to make your point, isn't it?"

"You're not dealing with your average guy, for sure."

"Look, can I leave you with this? I hear what you're saying, but I'd feel – we'd all feel – a lot safer if this went public."

"I'm going to have to find out more back-ground," Hampton told him. "You'll have to give me some time if I'm going to work on the story. Or would you sooner it went to another FNS writer?"

"No way. You were Charlie's writer, you're ours now. We want you."

"I'll look into it. That's all I can promise you right now. And if you find out any more, let me know. Here's my cellphone number. Don't call me from your turret – it'll be recorded."

"Teach your grandmother to suck eggs," Tommy said disgustedly. She hadn't heard the expression before, but guessed its meaning. "You know we always use cellphones to go off the re-cord." He stood up. "I'll be in touch."

Hampton watched as Tommy rejoined his group and talked animatedly, presumably telling them about the conversation he'd just had.

FIVE: AUGUST 2007

THE FIRST THING he was going to do as a civilian, Powers told himself, was to go to see his younger sister and her kids. There were four of them, and they all adored their Uncle Henry. There had been a father, but he'd left them some time ago, or to be more accurate, Laroche had thrown him out. As far as Powers knew, they hadn't officially divorced, and the ex- (for the life of him, Powers couldn't remember his name for a few minutes) wasn't sending any money to support his kids.

Powers, unmarried, unless you count being wedded to the Corps, had little on which he wanted to spend his major's pay. He saved some of it, and sent most of the rest to Laroche. A few years ago, she'd moved into an upmarket house in a new development. Personally, he considered that the house was too big and too extravagant for her, but it wasn't his business to interfere, and he knew that she would resent it if he did. Last leave, he'd visited her home for the first time since she had moved, and admired the spacious gleaming kitchen with all the modern appliances, the expensive wooden furniture, and the luxurious bathrooms. He asked himself how she'd been able to afford all of this on her income working at the call center, but when he'd tentatively raised the subject, she'd waved his worries away and told him that he was living in the past, and money was easy to come by now.

For a while, he wondered if she'd got herself mixed up in the drug business or something illegal, in which case he would certainly have put his foot down and spoken his mind. A little discreet investigation told him that this wasn't happening, much to his relief. He wasn't quite sure how he would have handled it. Fighting the Taliban in the Afghan mountains was one thing, but having a showdown with your feisty kid sister was quite another.

He entered the room where he was about to sign his resignation from the Corps, his heart pounding. For one crazy minute, he wondered whether to change his mind and sign on for another tour. Then he remembered the endless hours spent in the crazy landscape with the impossible weather. The strain of not knowing whether you were talking to a friend or an enemy. Whether they were going to throw a party for you with all the goat stew you could eat, or start throwing stones at you, or shoot you in the back, or explode some sort of home-made bomb under you. No way did he want any more of that.

But he'd miss the Corps, for sure.

He signed the papers.

"What are you going to do, now, Major?" asked the processing officer. "Got a job lined up? None of my business, I suppose, but I always like to know."

Powers shook his head. "Nothing lined up just yet. I'm going to take my time looking. Not even sure what part of the country I want to live in right now. One thing's for sure. I've had enough of rocks and mountains and deserts. Somewhere flat and green. And not too hot in the summer."

The other laughed. "I can understand how you feel. Good luck, sir. Semper fi."

"Semper fi," Powers replied. He wondered how long it would be before he felt he was a civilian again. It wasn't just a question of the uniform, but there was something more to it than that. It was feeling good about yourself, and your comrades, and the country you served. He'd never seen himself as a gung-ho type, but the quiet way he expressed his devotion to America had won him the nickname of "Major USA" among his fellow-officers, who were amused and respectful at the same time about his defense of the American ideals. Would that feeling ever go away?

He walked out of the building, and was amazed to find himself wiping a tear from his eye. Marines don't cry, he told himself. Even former Marines.

The flight to Akron, the nearest airport to his sister's house, took a few hours, giving him time to think and look around him. For some reason, he hadn't noticed before how large – well, fat was a better word – his fellow-Americans had become. After so long living with men in superb physical condition, in a country where most people barely had enough to eat, the idea of someone's body spilling over into the next airline seat, as his neighbor's was doing, was somewhat distasteful, almost nauseating. The way that he and his fellow-passengers were treated by the "security" forces at the airport (and he could find holes in their methods that you could drive a bus through) disgusted him. It reminded him of the way in which the worst of the American forces in Afghanistan treated the natives of the country – something he'd always put a stop to when he had had the authority to do so.

When he arrived at the other end, he rented a car (American, of course – he wasn't going to be driving a Toyota or a Honda) and drove out to the suburban development where his sister lived.

To his surprise, the house seemed to be deserted. There were no kids' toys out in the front yard, no curtains at the window, and when he passed the mailbox by the gate, it was overflowing. He emptied it, to discover it was almost all junk mail together with a few utility bills. He parked the car and walked to the front door. There was a notice there, which he read with horror, informing him that the bank had repossessed the house as a result of the occupier's being unable to meet the mortgage repayment schedule.

His first reaction was one of panic. Where was she? How in hell was he going to find her? Was she even in the same town?

Then came anger. What the hell? He'd been sending her enough money, hadn't he? Why hadn't she told him that she was in trouble? He knew she'd always been proud and more than a little ornery when it came to talking about money, but he was her brother, for Christ's sake. Couldn't she have told him?

He retraced his steps back to the car, and looked around the development. It seemed that Laroche's house was not the only empty one. About half the houses seemed to be unoccupied. The last time he'd visited, they'd all seemed to be full of happy families – a real community, in fact. What was going on?

He went over to one of the empty-looking houses, and saw the same notice that he'd seen on Laroche's door. It made no sense. How could a whole community fall behind on their payments like this? Had there been some sort of plague or something that he hadn't heard about?

The house next to the one where he was standing was occupied, by the look of it, and he went over and knocked on the door. A young woman, about the same age as Laroche, opened it. She looked at him, tall, fit, and still with his Marine haircut, and started to shut the door rapidly, but Powers was too quick for her, and stuck his foot out, preventing the door from closing.

"Sorry, ma'am," he said softly. "If I could just

ask you a few questions, please?"

"You're not from the bank?" she asked suspiciously. "Because if you are, you can fuck off and go to Hell."

"I'm not from the bank," he assured her. "I don't know how I can prove that, but I promise you that I'm not. I'm Laroche's brother. She used to live over there," pointing to the house, "but she's not there now, and I was wondering if you could help me and tell me where she is now."

"She never told you?" The young woman shook her head in disbelief.

"No. And all these other empty houses. Where is everybody? Last time I was here, it was all fine."

"When were you last here, then, mister?"

"A year ago. No, make that two."

"A lot's happened in those two years. Where have you been since then?"

"Afghanistan, mostly."

"Oh, you're a soldier?"

"No, ma'am, I was a Marine. I stopped being a Marine yesterday."

"Didn't your sister tell you what was going on?" she asked him. He shook his head. "Well, we've been screwed, mister. Every last one of us living here."

"What do you mean?"

"You'd better go and talk to the bank, Mister Marine. They'll tell you all about their little schemes. Try and sell you a house you can't afford."

"Any idea where my sister might be?"

She shrugged. He noticed her thin shoulders under the cotton T-shirt. As thin as some of the Afghanis that he'd been living among for the past few years. Pretty face, though, and looked as though she had brains with it. "No idea. Could be on the road."

"How do you mean, on the road? She's got kids."

"So have they all. Whole families living on the road, out of a car. Your sister got a man? Never saw one there, but you never know."

He shook his head. It was partly a gesture of negation, and partly one of disbelief. "No, no man that she ever told me about. There was one once."

"Guess there must have been one once if she's got kids. Look, mister," noticing the look on his face. "I'm sorry about your sister. This has got to be a shock. I'd invite you in to talk and for something to eat if I had anything in the house. But I don't have anything, honest to God." To his embarrassment, she started to cry. "I've got three kids myself and a useless man who can't seem to get himself a job. And no money. And letters all the time from the bank. They're going to throw us all out on the streets if we can't find the money. That is, if we don't starve to death first."

Holy shit, he thought to himself. This is America? He reached in his pocket and pulled out his billfold. "This any use to you?" he asked, holding out a hundred.

She looked at it, astounded, and pushed his

hand away roughly. "I wasn't begging, mister. Just telling it like it is, understand. Now just go away and leave us. You're OK, aren't you? Probably got a nice shiny pension from those Marine buddies of yours. All those veteran benefits I keep reading about." His foot was still in the door, so she couldn't shut it.

He took a deep breath and counted to ten before he answered. "I know you weren't begging," he said, as slowly and patiently as he could manage. "But you're in trouble, right?" She nodded. "You could be my sister. Sounds like it's just blind chance that you're here and she isn't. It could easily have been the other way around, I guess?" She nodded again. "And if it was my sister, I'd want to believe that some stranger would come along and want to help her a little, just like I want to help you a little. Okay?" She nodded a third time. "So, are you going to take this or not?"

She looked up at him with tears still running down her face. "I'll take it. You're a good man, Mister Marine. Hope you find your sister." Suddenly she put her arms around his waist and hugged him. "There should be more people in the world like you." She squeezed him tight, and then let go of him, and took the bill from his hand. "Just saying thanks isn't enough. I really wish I could help you find your sister. Like I say, I don't know where she might be, but you could start by going down the road into Akron, and talking to the bank there. There's quite a few of them along that road. You might be lucky and find her somewhere along there, or you might find someone who knows her and can tell you where she is. Now get your ass out of there before I start crying my eyes out again. Go with God, mister." He removed his foot, and she closed the door.

He went back to his sister's house and made a note of the bank's name and address before climbing into the car and setting off for central Akron. He didn't see anyone who looked like his sister. He found the bank without difficulty, and parked the car outside.

Major Henry Powers had never been one to shirk confronting authority, and he strode into the bank, consciously adopting the badass attitude which had put the fear of God into his platoon on those occasions when he had needed to do that.

"I want to see the manager who deals with home loans," he said to one of the tellers.

AFTER ABOUT TEN MINUTES' WAITING, Powers was shown into a small office, with a desk behind which sat a hard-faced woman in a dark gray "power" business suit. Christ, she was even wearing some sort of a tie, he thought to himself. To his eyes, she had bitch written all over her. Bottle blonde, and hair cut in a severe style. If she was wearing makeup, it was so subtle as to be almost unnoticeable. The nameplate on her desk informed him that he was meeting Leonora Allenby.

She remained seated as he entered the room and extended his hand across the desk. She didn't take it. Well, fuck you, lady, he thought to himself. He looked. No wedding ring. No surprise there.

"Take a seat, Mr.," she consulted the yellow sticky note on her desk. "Mr. Powers." There was more of a hint of a Southern accent. Not from this area, for sure.

Time to pull rank. "Actually, it's Major."

"Sorry?"

"My rank is Major. United States Marine Corps."

Cool bitch. Not a flicker of surprise. "Well, then, Major, if you prefer it. I don't believe you are one of our customers?" It was hardly a question.

"No." Damn it, if she wanted to play hard to get, so could he.

"Then how do you believe I can help you?"

"I would like to buy a mortgage."

"You mean you would like to take out a mortgage? To borrow money against a property?"

"No. I have a property in mind and I would like to buy the mortgage on it."

She sighed. "Then you will have to talk to the owner of the property."

"I believe I am doing so right now."

"Oh? Can you tell me where you are talking about?"

"3205 Willow Avenue."

She tapped away on her computer keyboard. "Yes, the original holder of the mortgage failed to meet the repayment schedule. The house is now vacant."

"Have you any idea where she might be?"

She laughed. He couldn't believe it. She actually laughed. "Mr. – sorry, Major – Powers, do you know how many houses we've had to repossess? It's not our business to keep an eye on all those deadbeats."

My sister is no deadbeat, he thought, but didn't say. "Any idea why you might have so many borrowers who couldn't keep up the payments?"

"Sure. They were lazy."

"You mean they had no jobs?"

"No. They didn't bother to read the terms of the mortgage. And then it bit them in the ass."

"Could you explain a bit further?"

"I'm a busy professional with a job to do, Major. I don't have time to waste on people who aren't even customers of the bank."

Jesus Christ, he thought to himself. If she were a man, he'd… He breathed in deeply, and the moment passed.

It seemed she had noticed his flash of anger, and she appeared to relent a little. "Look, here's a copy of the mortgage agreement that these people signed." She reached in her desk drawer, and handed him a thickish sheaf of papers. "Don't bother trying to read it now. You'll be here all day and most of the night. Now, if there's nothing more I can do for you…"

"Yes, I said that I wanted to buy the mortgage on that property, didn't I?"

"Well, you can't."

"Why not?"

"Because we don't own it any more. We sold it on."

"To whom?"

"How would I know? You'd have to ask someone in Finance in the head office in Columbus."

"Do you often sell off mortgages like this?"

She shrugged. "It's bank policy. Now if you're certain there's nothing else…"

"Thank you, no." He stood up, picking up the mortgage agreement, and opened the office door. She remained unmoving behind her desk. He went out of the office, and as he was about to close the door, his frustration boiled over. "And fuck you too, you cold-hearted bitch! Fuck you up the ass!" he shouted at her in his loudest Marine parade-ground tones, before slamming the door shut as hard as he could. The other workers in the open-plan office leading to Allenby's private office appeared above their cubicle dividers, like gophers popping out of their holes, with what looked like smirks on their faces. He heard a few giggles.

At least I made someone's day, he thought as he strode through the awed occupants of the cubicles, brandishing the printed mortgage agreement like a weapon. As he left the bank, the security guard, responding to some primeval instinct, actually saluted him, and he returned the gesture.

Once he was in his car he turned the ignition, and turned on the air-conditioning. Cool it, he told himself, breathing hard. Cool it. The Allenby woman had really annoyed him. Was reading legal documents a way of lowering your blood pressure? He'd never heard of it as a cure, but there was no harm in trying. He started to read the mortgage agreement, and gave up almost immediately. The type was so damn small it hurt his eyes. He had a feeling that even if he could read the words, he would hurt his brain trying to understand it. And that bitch said that the people who took out these mortgages were lazy? He'd bet money that she'd never read the thing herself. He had half a mind to read the thing through, memorize it, and ask her a few questions. Then ask her who was the lazy one. The self-proclaimed professional, or the poor suckers who'd been asked to sign their names at the bottom of an illegible sheaf of papers?

He found he was breathing hard again, as angry as he had ever been in his life. Was this the woman who'd actually been responsible for selling the mortgage to his sister, and then so casually washed her hands of any responsibility towards other human beings? He didn't know for sure, but he would bet that she was involved somehow.

Irrationally, he wished he was back in the Marines and could call in an airstrike on the enemy stronghold, for that's the way it seemed to him at that moment. Stop it, he told himself. This is America. This is your own country. These are your people. There's got to be some mistake here. Someone got the forms mixed up. Laroche was given the wrong forms to sign. No she wasn't, because everyone in that development was falling behind on their loans. Something very wrong going on there.

Anyway, time to find a motel and crash. He had to get to the state capital and find out what the hell had happened to Laroche's mortgage.

Some ribs and a few beers later, he was lying

on the motel bed, trying to make sense of what David Letterman was talking about. He'd been out of the country for too long to pick up all the references. Celebrity gossip bored him, in any case.

THE NEXT MORNING saw him up bright and early. Breakfast at a diner. He'd had worse breakfasts in his life, but they'd been MREs on top of a mountain in Afghanistan. He didn't think he'd ever paid for a worse breakfast. Watery scrambled eggs, half-cooked pancakes with fake syrup. To make up for the almost-raw pancakes, the bacon was cremated. The coffee was drinkable, at least by comparison with Afghan well water.

The waitress serving him looked tired and miserable. He tried a few jokes, but she didn't respond. Her mood matched the gray sky outside, and he was glad to get out of the place. He left an over-generous cash tip under his plate for her, though. Maybe it would cheer her up a little.

He pulled out of the parking lot and set his course for Interstate 71 to take him to Columbus. He'd gone about a mile when he saw a woman, dragging a wheeled suitcase, and three children, all carrying some sort of bag, walking by the side of the road. The woman looked familiar. He slowed as he passed them, and then stopped. It was the woman he'd talked to yesterday, and given the money to. She'd said she had a man, though. Where was he?

He opened the car door and called back to her.

"Who are you?" she asked, and then she appeared to recognize him. "Hey, it's Mr. Clean Marine from yesterday. What the hell are you still doing around here?"

"I'm on my way to Columbus. Where are you going?"

"To be honest, I have no fucking idea right now. It was only a couple of hours after you left us that the bastards came round and kicked us out of the house."

"Just like that?"

"Just like that, the cocksuckers." She seemed to have no inhibitions about her language in front of the children.

"What if you said you weren't going to leave?"

"Where in hell have you been?" She looked at him incredulously. "Oh yes, Afghanistan. Well, I don't know what they get up to there, but in the good old U S of A, you can go to jail for that sort of thing."

He digested her words for a moment. Probably she was wrong about that. That sort of thing just didn't happen.

"Well, they must have given you some papers when they came round, right?"

"Yeah."

"They'd tell you your rights. They can't just kick you out of the house like that."

She looked at him. "Listen, Mister Marine. You're a big tough guy, right? You're used to tearing up telephone books with your bare hands, and that kind of crap, right? Well, me, I'm just a mother with three kids and a useless man. Five foot something, and I'm not going to tell you what I weigh, but it's probably the same as one of your legs."

"So?"

"So you might be able to face off against a couple of six-foot-two, two-hundred-pound assholes shouting in your face and waving papers at you. No way can I stand up to them and not risk getting hurt. And then what happens to the kids if I get hurt?"

"Couldn't you call someone? Say, your pastor?"

"Don't talk to me about that creep. I called him, and all he could say was that I'd broken my word and I must take the consequences. I knew I was in arrears over the mortgage and I owed them more money than I can pay. I know they can take your house away if you don't pay. I've heard of it happening. Hell, I've seen it happen. Anyway, even if I could fight them in court, who's going to pay for my lawyer? And then I've got to pay the mortgage. Where's that money going to come from? Eh? So I threw away those fucking papers. I guess we could go back and look for them, but they'll be over half the state by now."

"Okay, you've made your point."

She stood silently looking at him. He got the impression he was being judged.

"Anyway," he said to her. "I'm going this way, and it looks as though you are, too. Want a lift?"

"What, all of us?" she said.

"Of course."

"Where to?"

"Where do you want to go? You're walking to somewhere, aren't you?"

"Walking away, more like."

"Not going anywhere, then?"

"Well, if I'm going anywhere, I suppose it's Wilmington. To my sister's. God knows how we're going to get there, but it's about all I've got."

"Then that's where we're going."

"But it's a long way past Columbus. Nearly two hundred miles from here, for God's sake."

"So what? That's where we're going to go," he repeated. He popped the trunk.

"Jesus, you're a good man. Okay, you kids, put your bags in the trunk and get into the back. Don't make a mess of the man's car, okay?"

The children appeared to be aged between about nine and five. They were shabbily dressed, but their clothes were clean, and they appeared healthy, if skinny.

"You said we weren't to get in a car with strangers," said the eldest, a girl.

"It's all right if I'm with you, Lisa," her mother reassured her. "Never get in a car with a stranger if I'm not with you."

"What about if Dad's with us?" asked the middle boy.

"Dad won't be with you ever again," she said shortly. She turned to Powers. "Chickenshit bastard took the car and ran off as soon as he could. And he took the hundred you gave me. Bastard."

"Don't you think he'll be back?"

"Wouldn't take him back if he came crawling back on his fucking hands and knees, useless piece of shit."

"You tell us not to use those words," said Lisa.

She groaned. "I can use them, you can't. And before you ask, it's because I say so." Powers smiled to himself. "And you can stop grinning," she told him. "Got kids?" He shook his head. "Then don't say anything."

"I wasn't going to," he said. "By the way, I'm Henry."

"I'm Jeanine, and these are Lisa, Tyrone, and Kareema."

"Good to know you, Jeanine. You guys comfortable?" he called to the back seat. There was a chorus of "yes", and he put his foot on the gas.

"Why are you doing this?" asked Jeanine after a couple of miles. "What's in it for you?"

He thought about it for a while. "There's nothing in it for me except what's in it for anyone who helps another person. Why am I doing it? Guess I'm a nice guy."

"Well, you don't look like one of those serial killers you see on the news, for sure."

"I am a serial killer, though," he told her.

"You're joking. I hope," she added. She sounded nervous.

"That's what I did in the Marines. That was my job."

"Oh." She appeared to relax – a little. "I guess you're right, though. Funny, you never really think of things that way."

"I do," he said. "And I think that's one of the reasons why I'm not in the Corps any more."

"Well, you're certainly different," she said. They drove on for a few more miles. "Where did you go after you left us yesterday? Did you get to the bank in Akron? See anyone?"

"Yes." He told her about his meeting with Leonora Allenby.

"She's a bitch, that woman," said Jeanine.

"You know her? Friend of yours?"

"Hardly. She was the bank's person in the room when we signed the mortgage papers, though."

"Papers like this?" He showed her the sheaf of papers he'd been given the previous day.

"I guess so, without busting my eyes trying to read twenty pages of small print that no-one except a lawyer can understand. It looks like what we signed."

"She said that all you people were lazy not to read it."

"And you said?"

"I didn't say it, I shouted it so the whole office could hear. And I am not going to repeat what I said in front of your children."

"Mom uses those words all the time," said

Lisa, who'd obviously been following their conversation.

"Doesn't mean I'm going to use them," said Powers, smiling. He looked over at Jeanine, who was smiling, too.

"You're all right, Henry," she said to him, and patted his arm.

"Did you know that the bank sold your mortgages on to someone else?"

"No. Who?"

"Allenby didn't know or wouldn't tell me. That's what I want to find out in Columbus."

"Mind if we come with you? I'd be interested in knowing the answer to that myself."

"Your sister?"

"She can wait, I guess. Turn here for I-71."

"Thanks. By the way, who sold you the mortgage? Allenby?"

"No way. She wouldn't get her hands dirty with actually selling something. No, it was some slimy little prick—"

"Mom!" from the back seat.

"All right, sweetie. Some slimy little person. He said he was from the realtors, but I never saw him in there the other times."

"Would he have sold my sister her mortgage?"

"Who knows? Maybe."

"Got a name?"

"Better than that. I got a card. Somewhere with me in that case."

"You've called him?"

"Sure. And he just laughed. Told me that his job

ended as soon as I signed the papers. After that I was on my own, he said."

"I think I might pay a call on him some time. Might end up doing more than just shouting out a string of four-letter words."

"I'd like to be with you when that happens."

They drove on for about twenty minutes and there was a wail from the back. "Mom, I need to go to the bathroom."

"Okay, sweetie, I hear you."

"We'll pull over at the next place along the way."

"That'll be Ashland. When did you guys last eat?"

"Don't ask," Jeanine warned him.

"Then we'll find somewhere for us."

They found a Perkin's on the road into Ashland, and the kids dashed for the bathroom while Henry and Jeanine found a table.

"You do know we've got no money?" she warned him. "Well, maybe a little, but not enough for more than a doughnut between the four of us."

"I'm paying," he told her. "And no arguments," putting up a warning hand. "I want to do this, okay? I told you why yesterday."

"What do you want from me in return?"

"Not what I suspect you're thinking." He frowned. "What can you give me in return? Company, for one. And I need you to explain things to me."

"Me, explain to you?" She laughed. "Mister

Marine, you strike me as a damn' sight smarter than me, just by looking at you. Though I admit you seem pretty dumb at times."

"That's what I mean. I've been out of things for so long. Being in the military, and out of the country, you're living in a different world a lot of the time."

"Okay, I'll be your jungle guide. And believe me, it really is a fucking jungle out there sometimes." The children came out of the bathroom. "Let's see your hands. All washed and clean? Well done."

The children all chose pancakes. Henry selected the full breakfast with hash browns, which he hoped would compensate for the lousy meal he'd had earlier, and Jeanine simply ordered an English muffin.

"You should eat more than that," he told her. "That's an order." He smiled to take the sting out of his words.

"I'm not one of your Marines," she retorted, but added a cinnamon roll to her order.

The food arrived, and the pancakes started to disappear fast.

"Thank you, Mr. Marine," Lisa said to him as the last drop of syrup got mopped up with the last shred of pancake.

"I'm Henry," he smiled at her.

"Thank you, Henry," from the other two.

"You guys go to the bathroom before we set off again," their mother told them.

"Nice kids," he said to her as they trotted off.

"I try," she answered. "It's tough. Not because of them, you understand. They really are great kids, though. How many has your sister got?"

"You remembered? Four. I guess they're all a bit older than yours, but only by a year or so. Two boys and then two girls. They're great kids, too."

"Wish you had kids of your own?"

The question caught him off balance. "I guess I would like that, if they had the right mother." He smiled at her.

"What's that smile meant to mean?"

"Nothing. Just day-dreaming, I guess."

"I'm frightened to ask any more questions." But it was said with an answering smile.

He paid the check, and the kids returned from the bathroom.

On the road to Columbus, Henry taught the children some of the cleaner songs that he'd sung with his fellow Marines, and they cheerfully belted out "Itsy Bitsy Spider" and "Yankee Doodle", with his baritone underlaying their piping trebles. Jeanine sat silently with her arms folded for the first couple of songs, but ended up joining in the chorus of the third song, "Amazing Grace", and all the others, until he started on "From the halls of Montezuma".

"No, please," she said. "I don't want them to grow up with that sort of thing."

He gripped the wheel tightly in a reflex anger. "What sort of thing?"

"Fighting. War. My country right or wrong sort of thing." She sounded angry. "Look, it's nothing personal, okay? You're a good, kind man from all that I've seen of you so far. You're great with the kids. There's just so much crap out there that I don't want them to get mixed up in." She sniffed. "I'm going to tell you something, because I know you'll react the right way. I used to have two brothers, both a bit older than me. They're dead now." She sniffed again.

He kept his eyes on the road. He'd been through this in the Marines several times, when members of his platoon had come to confide something to him; the sort of thing that they could trust only an officer to understand. The best way to help in these cases was to act as he was doing now. "I'm listening."

There was a long pause. "One of them died in a gang war. Shot. And the other was killed by the police. They said he was 'resisting arrest'. Complete load of crap. How do you resist arrest when you've been Maced and handcuffed?"

He didn't dare to look at her, frightened that she was going to break down completely. "I hear you," he said softly. "I'm sorry to hear that. I know these things happen, but I've never met it at first hand, as it were, like this. I believe you, Jeanine. Truly, I believe you."

"Thank you," she said. "Somehow I don't think you're the sort of man who'd say that just to keep a woman quiet."

There was silence for a while, which he broke by starting up with "Ten Green Bottles," and the children joined in.

They reached the outskirts of Columbus. "Head for downtown?" he asked.

"I guess. Never been there before, but that's where the banks are."

The bank was impossible to miss. A gleaming modern glass-covered cube with the bank's logo and name plastered in large letters at the top, near the state Capitol.

"Wonder who paid for all that?" she said bitterly.

"Are you coming in with me?" he asked her, while he was looking for a place to park the car.

"I'll stay with the children. I saw a sign to the art museum. Maybe you can drop us off there."

"Art museum?"

"Yeah. I took art history a couple of years at college. Loved that shit. Still do."

"Sure, if that's what you want to do."

"Good for the kids, too," she said, as he pulled up outside the museum. "Are we going to see you again, I wonder?"

"Sure you are. Let's meet back here at two? I'll be stopped right here waiting for you," he said. "Need some money for lunch and things?" He peeled off a few more bills.

"Look, I don't know why you're doing this, but you don't have to, you know."

He laughed. "I don't know, either. Look, just take it, okay? Makes me feel good."

"You must be made of money."

"I'm not poor, put it that way. Anyway, remember, I've got all your things in the trunk."

She laughed back at him. "Sure. See you here at two. Lisa, Tyrone, Kareema, come on."

ONCE INSIDE THE BANK, he had to fight his way past the receptionist. Even after he'd given Leonora Allenby's name, and used his officer's rank to impress and intimidate, he found himself waiting in a brightly lit reception area, until "someone from Finance" deigned to see him.

The interior of the building was obviously designed to impress. In the usual run of things it would have impressed Powers, but after Jeanine's comment about who'd paid for it all, he was a little less than happy to see the large abstract oil paintings on the walls, and the hardwood furnishings. The coffee he was given while he was waiting was good, though, he had to admit. Funny, he'd never really asked himself how companies paid for all this eye candy. If it was a bank, he guessed it was from the bank's profits. But where did a bank's profits come from? Mortgages?

And not just the ordinary interest that the bank's customers were paying on the mortgages, it seemed. Not if the bank was repossessing houses at the rate it seemed was happening. And not if they were selling on these mortgages to…

The door opened, and the secretary who'd shown him in told him that a Mr. Tallman would see him now.

Mr. Francis Tallman turned out to be what Powers tended to think of as an all-American asshole. White, of course, seemingly quite a lot younger than Powers, and filled with his own importance. There weren't too many of that type in the Corps, but he'd met them in the other services, and they always put his back up. Despite his name, Mr. Tallman was actually quite short and Powers towered over him.

"And what can I do for you, Major?" asked the little blond squirt.

"I've been looking for my sister. She bought a house near Akron – Summit County – and she obviously fell behind on her payments. The property was repossessed."

"You should be talking to the Loans Department of the branch that sold her the mortgage, then, if you have a query. I am sorry you wasted your time coming here."

"I did talk to a Ms. Allenby there and she directed me here."

"Oh?"

"I wanted to buy my sister's mortgage, but she told me the bank no longer had it on its books."

"Without seeing the details, I would imagine that would be the case."

"Can you tell me who would have bought it?"

"Without knowing the details, it would be impossible to tell you, but it would have gone to one of the Wall Street firms. Maybe Lehman Brothers, or possibly Merrill Lynch."

"Why on earth would they be interested in buying my sister's mortgage?" Powers was genuinely puzzled.

"It wouldn't have been just your sister's mortgage that we sold on, of course. It would have been sold together with a few hundred others."

"So if I want my sister's mortgage, I must go to Wall Street?"

"In a nutshell, Major, yes."

"And why would Wall Street want these mortgages?"

"Are you an expert in finance, Major?" Each time he pronounced Powers' rank, he made it sound like an insult. "No? Then I am afraid there is no simple way to explain it."

Arrogant little prick, Powers thought to himself. "Try me."

"The Wall Street firms are selling the mortgages to other people. They take the mortgages off our hands, and sell them on to other people. They bundle them up and sell them as bonds."

"Hang on a moment. You're telling me that you're selling these mortgages on to the Wall Street banks?" Tallman agreed. "And then these Wall Street banks are selling them on to other people? I take out a mortgage with your bank, but you're not taking the risk any more. It's not your debt, because it's just being sold on?"

"Well, it's more complex than that, but that's the basic idea. The Wall Street guys bundle them up into CDOs."

"What the fuck's that when it's at home?"

Tallman frowned. "Listen, Major, I don't like your language."

"And I don't like yours. Stop trying to bullshit me and tell me in plain English what's going on, okay? And they can find buyers? Who?"

"Seems they can. Foreign banks, pension funds, and so on. Do you really want to know this?"

"Yes, I do. My family's involved." Powers leaned forward, so he was almost eyeball to eyeball with the banker, who flinched away from the menace of this big man.

"Okay, take it easy, will you? They're not selling individual mortgages, right? We're talking millions – billions of dollars here. Like I say, they bundle them all together and call them CDOs. That's Collaterialized Debt Obligations if you want it in full. Some are going to fail, sure, and some aren't. They set things up and bundle them together so that the risk is minimized." Powers frowned. "That's risk to Wall Street and the people buying these CDOs, not risk to the poor suckers who took out the mortgages."

"Why do you say 'suckers'? Why do they believe decent hard-working people like my sister will not be able to meet their obligations?"

"If you look at those mortgages, they're pretty much set up to fail. You people never seem to bother reading the small print."The little bastard seemed to be almost smirking.

"So you're telling me that your bank sells mortgages to people – my people – knowing that they will default on them— that's the word you people use? — and then you wash your hands of them by selling them on to bigger crooks on Wall Street?" Powers' voice had become louder and his tone had become angrier as he spoke, and Tallman started to shrink back in his chair. "Yes or no?" By now, Powers had stood up, and was towering over the cringing Tallman. "Yes or no, sonny?"

There was no answer. Powers bent forward and grabbed Tallman's lapels and dragged him to his feet. "Yes or no?" he bellowed into Tallman's face, channelling the drill instructors at Parris Island.

"Yes," came the meek answer, as Powers lifted the employee so that he was now standing on tip-toe. "This is assault – I hope you realize I could have you arrested for this."

"And you, sonny, are the lowest of the low. I hope you realize that. Scum is too good a word for you, you fucking crook," Powers said in a menacingly low voice, but he released his grip on the other's jacket, letting him drop. Tallman's knees buckled and he slumped to the ground. "And I don't know if you noticed, kid, but you just pissed yourself."

Without another word, he walked out of the room, and mashed the buttons on the elevator to take him down to the lobby. As he got out at the first floor, he was approached by a security guard. Obviously Tallman had phoned ahead.

"Come quietly now, and there'll be no trouble," the guard said to him. He took a closer look at Powers. "Holy shit, sir!" he said.

"Harriman. What the hell are you doing here? This is what you do now you've left the Corps? Threaten your old platoon officer with arrest?"

"Yes, sir. I mean no, sir. Just get your ass out of here now, and I'll tell them I was too slow. Di di mau. Sir."

"Semper fi, Harriman. And thanks."

He ran as fast as he could towards the lot where he had parked the car, and looked at his watch. Another twenty minutes before he was meant to be meeting Jeanine. Best just to drive around the corner, and hide in the car somewhere until it was time for her and the kids to come out of the museum.

Thought was action, and he spent the next twenty minutes hunkered down, hopefully out of sight, with the car parked in a side street between the hospital and the cathedral. Just before two, he started the car. Thank goodness. He could see Jeanine and the children waiting outside the museum. He made a U-turn, ignoring the blaring horns of protest from the other drivers, and pulled up beside the family.

"All get in, quick," he said.

"What's going on?" Jeanine said, but she bundled the kids into the back seat, and buckled her seatbelt as he stomped on the gas and the car took off down East Broad Street. "Hey! What's the big hurry?"

"I'm in deep shit," he confessed, as he turned right.

"And we are too, then, since we're with you? Well, thank you very much, my friend."

He shook his head. "No way would you be in trouble, but I don't want you to get involved in this at all."

"What the hell happened?"

"I lost it," he confessed. "There was some little prick—"There were gasps and giggles from behind him. "Sorry, kids. Sorry, Jeanine." He took a breath and started again. "This guy in the bank told me that these mortgages were set up to fail. They were meant to go wrong."

"I'd guessed something like that."

"And the banks are selling them on to Wall Street banks, who put them all together and sell them to other places like pension funds and so on. They couldn't give a flying—" He stopped, remembering the children. "They could care less about people like you and my sister."

"And?"

"And I lost it," he repeated. "I picked up the guy and shook him. He pissed his pants." More giggles from the back seat. "He wanted to have me arrested, but the security guard in the lobby was one of my platoon way back when, and let me get away. Lucky break."

"Sure, lucky. Now what?"

"We have two choices. One, I can take you on

to Wilmington, and drop you off at your sister's, like I was going to do. Two, we can go back to Akron and find my sister, and the guy who sold you the mortgage."

"Three," she said, "you can let us out of the car right here and now and we can make our own way to Wilmington. Four, we can go to Wilmington, drop off the kids to stay with Aunty Brandi, and I go back with you to find your sister and that guy."

"I want to stay with Aunty Brandi," said Tyrone. "She makes great chicken." There was a chorus of agreement.

"So it looks like Wilmington," said Powers. "Even if I didn't want to, I'd be outvoted. But Jeanine, you don't have to come with me looking for my sister if you don't want to."

"I know that. You don't have to take us to Wilmington, either."

"I want to help you," was all he could say at that point.

"Maybe I want to help you," she answered him.

"Fair enough." He took I-71 south to Wilmington.

Aunty Brandi turned out to be a slightly older version of Jeanine, with the same face, but a little more rounded in every area. Where Jeanine had angles, Brandi had curves. And where Jeanine had curves (and he couldn't help noticing that she did), Brandi's curves were softer. As he watched Brandi scoop up the kids into her arms, Powers felt a tug at his heartstrings for Laroche and her kids. He noticed Jeanine studying his face.

"Hurts, does it?" she said, sympathetically. "These could be your sister's kids, right?"

He said nothing, but simply nodded, a lump in his throat. They took the children's cases from the car, and Jeanine removed some children's clothes and toys out of her case before closing the lid and putting it back in the trunk.

"When will you be coming back?" Brandi asked.

Jeanine looked at Powers.

"Inside a week," he said. "Depends on a lot of things, but not more than a week."

"No problem," said Brandi. "It's going to be great having my three little darlings to stay. Louie and I never had kids of our own," she explained to Powers. "So I love these three as if they were my own."

"Don't you go spoiling them, now," said Jeanine. "Don't you go serving that chicken of yours at every meal, or they won't want to eat anything else when they come back to me. And ice-cream only once a day, mind."

"Yes, ma'am." Brandi dropped her voice, but Powers guessed he was meant to overhear the words. "I like your new man."

"He is not——" said Jeanine, and then stopped. "Oh, never mind."

"Okay, let's be off," said Powers, trying to salvage the situation.

"Sure. Bye, kids," picking each one up in turn and kissing them. "Be good. Don't go giving Aunt any trouble, you hear?"

"We'll be good," said Lisa.

"And we won't have chicken every meal," said Tyrone. "At least, not breakfast."

"You can have chicken for breakfast if you want it, honey," his aunt told him. Jeanine shot her a look. "But if you have it for breakfast, you can't have it again that day."

Powers smiled as he got into the car and Jeanine joined him. "You're a good mother to them," he told her.

"I try," she said. "It's hard sometimes with a useless man laying about the house."

There was silence between them for about twenty miles as they drove up back towards Akron. Somehow when they had been with the children, it seemed to have made conversation easier.

"What are we looking for?"

"Uh?"

"Your sister. What sort of car? Four kids? A bit older than mine? Anything else special? She have a wooden leg or something?"

Despite himself, he laughed. "No, there's no wooden leg. I think she was driving a gray Corolla last time I looked. She didn't mention that she'd changed it, but she might have done."

"What year? The car, I mean?"

"No idea. There's no way I could know that sort of thing, being out of the country."

"Guess so. So, no wooden leg, eh? That's going to make life difficult. What does she look like?"

"Taller than you, shorter than me. Last time

I saw her she had her hair in braids, but that doesn't mean a lot, does it?" He wriggled in his seat, and pulled his billfold out of his hip pocket and opened it. "Here," he said, passing a couple of photos over.

"Hey! Cute kids!"

He smiled. "They are, aren't they?"

"And that's your sister? I can see the family resemblance. Yeah, I seem to recognize her. Seen her around the place from time to time, but never spoke to her. When were these taken?"

"The last time I was here. Three years ago."

"You haven't seen her in three years?"

"Through the Internet. Skype and that sort of thing. She hasn't changed that much since that photo was taken, except her hair was in braids, like I said. Kids are three years older. I've got a photo on my laptop that she sent me a month or so back. We can show that to the police."

She shook her head. "Uh-huh. No police."

"Why? You're not hiding anything, are you?"

"I'm not, but you are. Why the hell else did we get out of Columbus so fast?"

"Okay, point taken."

"And you don't honestly think they'd help you, do you? Yeah, I know my family's had a bad experience with them, and I'm biased against them and all that shit, but trust me on this one. They wouldn't give a shit about finding your sister. There's hundreds like her, just in this state alone."

"I'd like to think you're wrong about that, but I have this feeling you're probably right."

"Thanks for believing me. Mind if we have the radio on?"

"Go ahead."

"What do you want to listen to?"

"Your choice. Surprise me." A minute later. "Yes, I am surprised," as the sound of a Mozart piano concerto filled the car.

"You mind?"

"No, not really. Just surprised, that's all."

The Mozart washed over them for a few miles, Jeanine humming along to herself. "Did you hear what Brandi said?" she asked him suddenly.

"About the chicken?"

"No, about you and me."

"I think I was meant to hear, wasn't I?"

"I don't know whether to be insulted or flattered by you."

"How do you mean?"

"I mean that you haven't shown the slightest interest in me that I can tell. Either I'm really insulted, because I don't think of myself as being that ugly, you know, or I'm really flattered that you treat me as an intelligent independent person and not just someone to jump into bed with. I'm guessing you're not gay, though I guess there may be such a thing as a gay Marine."

He sighed. "You're asking questions I really don't want to answer right now. But if it makes you feel good, I do see you as an intelligent independent person, I do find you attractive, and I don't usually jump into bed with people I've only known a couple of days. And no, I'm not gay, and yes, there are gay Marines."

"That answers all that, then, doesn't it?" she said.

"Let's change the subject," he said, after an awkward silence. "Tell me about the scumbag who was selling the mortgages. Who is he or was he?"

"If you can believe it, he was working with the pastor at the church."

"You mean the church was selling the mortgages?"

"Not directly, but this James Payton was working with the pastor. Every Sunday, we'd hear from the pastor how blessed we were to have in the congregation someone who could open the gates to owning our own home. He made it sound like opening the gates of Heaven."

"Uh-huh."

"You go to church, Henry?"

He laughed. "I used to. Of course, you get a lot of religion in the Corps, but it's not something you have a lot of choice about most of the time."

"Anyway, he opened up his shop on Sundays after service. Did a lot of business."

"Did he only work with the one church? This is the Church of Jesus Christ in Summit County?"

She nodded. "That's the one. Guess I might even have seen your sister there sometimes."

"So do we see the pastor or the scumbag first? Though I'm guessing that the pastor's more than a bit of a scumbag himself."

"Scumbag every time for me."

"Fine."

"Want to see him tonight?"

"Sure."

"Great. You can get us there?"

However, when they arrived at the church where Jeanine had said he did most of his business, all the lights were off, and there was no-one to be seen.

"Then we'll try him at home," said Jeanine. "I know where he used to live, anyway."

"Got his home address?"

She read it out from the card.

NINE: AUGUST 2007

A PORSCHE BOXTER and a black Hummer were parked outside the house where she took him. "Someone's doing well for themselves," Powers remarked as they parked the hire car in the road outside the house. They rang the doorbell, but there was no answer. They could hear squeals, almost screams, through the door. Powers looked at Jeanine. "What is going on?"

She shrugged. They rang the doorbell again and knocked, but there was no sign that they had been heard.

"We're going in," Powers told her. "Something really weird's going on in there. Listen. That's a child in some sort of pain. Stand back." He took a few steps back and then suddenly lunged forward, bringing his foot up and slamming it hard against the lock of the door, which burst open.

"Neat, huh? One of those things they teach you in the Marines?"

"Yep," he said. They walked in and followed the

sound of the screams down to a darkened den, with one wall dominated by an enormous flat-screen TV. Two overweight men were sprawled on the couch facing it. Neither was wearing pants. Lines and piles of white powder lay on the glass table in front of the couch. They were watching… Powers followed their gaze, and saw—

"Jesus fucking Christ!" he exploded. "You sick motherfuckers!" He looked around, picked up a heavy glass ashtray that was lying on the table, and hurled it with all his strength at the TV screen. There was a crash, a bang, and a shower of sparks. The room went almost completely dark. Powers reached out and turned on the ceiling light.

The larger of the two men on the couch spoke. "You shouldn't have done that," he said in a slow lazy voice. "We were just beginning to enjoy the evening."

"You sick fucks," Powers told them. "I've sometimes wondered what sort of lowlife gets his kicks from watching movies of kids being abused like that. Now I know. I hope you didn't see any of what was on that screen, Jeanine."

"I did, and I wish to God I hadn't," she said. "It will be with me to the end of my days." Her voice was shaking, and her body was rigid. "Pastor Davis, you can be sure the congregation will know about this as soon as we leave this place. And as for you, James Payton…"

"Now then, Sister Jeanine, don't be stupid. It's the word of your pastor against you. I understand you lost your home the other day. You're upset. You're emotional. Who's going to believe you and this gorilla here?"

"'This gorilla here', as you call him, is a Major in the Marine Corps." A look of fear crossed the pastor's face. "I think people might just believe him."

"Okay, okay, let's be cool about this," said the other man. His voice was harsh and penetrating where the pastor's was smooth and oily. "How much?" he said to Powers.

"How much what?" asked Powers.

"How much money do you want to keep quiet about this, of course?"

"There's not enough money in the world to keep my mouth shut about this. Try again."

"Well, maybe this will persuade you," said Payton. Somewhere among the cushions on the couch there had been a Colt .45 automatic, which he now held pointed at Powers.

"Oh, for Christ's sake," said Powers, taking a stride forward and twisting the gun out of the other's hand. "If you're going to threaten someone with a gun, at least take the safety off." He did so, and pointed the gun at the terrified Payton, who slowly raised his hands in the air.

"How did you know it was safe?" asked Jeanine, obviously impressed.

"Been working with these babies for quite a few years now." He turned to the two men on the couch. "I see you've taken off your pants to be comfortable. Let's get really comfortable, shall we? Take off your undershorts."

"You can't do this," protested the pastor. "What the hell are you going to do to us?"

"I hope you're not trying to argue." There was steel in Powers' voice. Payton had already removed his underwear. "Throw the shorts over there," Powers told him, "and keep your hands away from your crotch."

"Can I twist his balls off?" Jeanine asked Powers.

"Not yet. We'll save that for later. Hurry up, pastor, we haven't got all night. That's better. Toss them over there. Hands on your heads, both of you."

As Powers had intended, the two men were now completely humiliated and vulnerable, each with his penis and testicles exposed, and their hands unable to cover them.

"What do you want?" the pastor asked. All the fight seemed to have gone out of him.

"Something that seems to have been missing from round here for some time. The truth about the mortgages that you were selling."

"You mean the subprimes," said Payton. "The ones that I was selling in the church."

"The ones you were selling in the church, yes. Go on."

"There was no way that those mortgages could be repaid. I was making up the income figures on the forms. This one here," starting to point at Jeanine, but stopping abruptly as the pistol moved to point at his groin, "could never have paid the installments, even if they'd stayed the same all the way through."

"How do you mean?"

"A teaser mortgage. Low interest rates for the first few years, shoot up after that. All in the small print. Page seven, if I remember right," he smirked

"That's right," said Jeanine. "Suddenly the payments just went through the roof – two or three times what we had been paying. There was no way we could afford to keep that sort of thing going. But I didn't understand why. Every time I tried to talk to someone in the bank, they were busy. I must have called a dozen times. And you, you miserable fucker," addressing Payton, "were no help at all."

"Not my job after I sold the mortgage," said Payton. He shrugged as best he could.

"I can see you got paid quite a commission out of it all. Hummers and Porsches and lines of coke and a nice big home theater system to watch your filth on. And you, pastor, presumably got your cut for opening the gates of Paradise for your flock. From this slimeball here?"

"From the bank," the pastor said. His voice was shaking, and he appeared to be about to burst into tears. "Can I put my hands down now? Please?"

"No, keep them up there. Who were you dealing with in the bank? What was their name?"

"Allenby. Leonora Allenby."

"Why is that not a surprise to me?" Powers said. "Jeanine, you wanted to twist this one's balls off?"

"No," wailed Payton. Powers stepped forward and put the muzzle of the gun to his temple. The pastor watched in sick fascination as Jeanine moved in front of Payton, and put her hand between his legs. His face twisted in sudden agony, and he let out a scream.

"Enjoying this?" Powers asked the pastor. "You seemed to be enjoying watching this sort of thing happening to the kids in the video. Not so much fun when it happens to a friend of yours, is it? Keep your fucking hands on your head!" he ordered the writhing Payton, jabbing the pistol against his temple. "Don't worry about your balls. You're not going to need them for much longer. Just think of this as a temporary inconvenience."

Jeanine must have done something out of the ordinary. Payton's eyes rolled back in his head, he let out a high-pitched scream, and fell back, seemingly unconscious.

"Dear God in Heaven, what did you do to him?" asked the pastor. "Are you going to do that to me?"

"I must have squeezed too hard," she said. "I think I felt something pop."

Powers felt sick just thinking about it, but the pastor suddenly vomited explosively over himself. "Can I clean myself up?"

"No need for that," said Powers. "Jeanine, you want to start on this one?" The pastor heaved again.

"No, please, anything but that."

"I can think of much worse things than that,"

said Powers. "I've been in Afghanistan, after all. Do you want to hear what the women did to one of our men who they captured?"

"Noooo," wailed the pastor.

"Jeanine, go upstairs and out of the house and get in the car. Don't argue. Do it."

She seemed about to argue, but took one look at his face, and left the room.

"What are you going to do?"

"No, it's what you're going to do," Powers told him. "First, if there's any religion left in you at all, you can say your prayers, though it seems to me that you sold your soul to the devil a long time ago. I'll give you a minute." He ostentatiously looked at his watch. "Okay, time's up," he said after a minute. "Now I want you to do something for me." He explained what he wanted the pastor to do. "It's really quite simple. You might even enjoy it."

"I can't do that."

"I think you can do it quite easily," Powers told him, kicking him hard on the kneecap. "I'm sure you won't find it that hard." He kicked the other kneecap. "See?" he said, as the pastor grovelled into position.

"You really want me to do that?"

"Not really what I want. It's what you're going to have to do."

The pastor, with a look of frozen disgust on his face, repeated his plea. "I can't do it!"

"I think you can," Powers repeated. "With just

a little encouragement." He rested the muzzle of the pistol against the back of the pastor's neck. "There you go," as the pastor reluctantly carried out his orders.

Powers fired twice in quick succession, and his victim's body went limp. Powers moved the gun to point at Payton, and put two shots into his right temple.

He left the room, turning off the light as he did so, and hurried upstairs.

Jeanine was waiting in the car. "I heard shots," she said. "What happened?"

"You don't want to know," he told her. "They're both dead, and I can be pretty certain that the details aren't going to be splashed all over the newspapers. Lines of coke all over the place, child snuff porn on the DVD player, no pants or undershorts on either of them, one of them with crushed balls, and there's a little extra twist I came up with."

"You what?"

"And a couple of .45s in the head of each," he concluded, avoiding her question. "You reckon the local paper's going to cover that one?"

"You're insane," she said, and suddenly giggled.

"You're not too sane yourself," he said. "Come on, let's get out of here and find a motel for the night."

"You're not suggesting…?"

"I'm suggesting nothing, except we find a room, or two rooms if you prefer, get something to eat, and go to sleep."

THEY FOUND A MOTEL, and somewhat to Powers' surprise, Jeanine offered to share the double room with him.

"It doesn't necessarily mean anything," she said. "Just as long as you realize that."

The room was depressing. Somehow, everything in it seemed to have had the color sucked out. The bed was hard, but at least there were no bedbugs to be seen when he pulled down the covers to check.

"You were expecting some?" she asked when he explained.

"Overseas, bedbugs would be a welcome change. You wouldn't believe some of the things that have wanted to share the bed with me. Some had a lot more than two legs, and some didn't have any."

"Yech. I hate those things."

"Want to get out of this place and eat?"

"I'm not hungry. Kinda lost my appetite."

"Me too."

"Want me to get a few brews and some chips or something, then? I saw a 7-11 just down the road."

"Diet Coke for me. I don't drink beer on a first date." She smiled. "And yeah, some chips."

He returned a few minutes later with a couple of large bottles of cola and a some bags of chips.

"Not exactly a healthy balanced diet," he remarked. "But I decided beer wasn't a good idea for me either. Not tonight."

"I don't feel that healthy or balanced myself," she said. "I feel dirty and unclean. Look, this is going to sound crazy, but would you mind going to the bathroom and chasing out any spiders you see in the shower? I see one of those babies, and I freak out. At home, I get— I mean I got— the kids to do that. Every time."

He dutifully checked the shower, and reported that the room was free of eight-legged intruders.

She rummaged in her suitcase for a change of clothes, and disappeared into the bathroom with them. Powers lay on the bed, and flicked his way through the TV channels, sipping a large non-diet Coke, and working his way through a bag of corn chips.

Jeanine emerged, her hair in a towel, and wearing a flimsy teddy. Without speaking, he poured her a diet Coke, and passed the bag of chips over to her.

"Thanks. What's the crap you've got on the TV?"

"No idea. Change the channel or turn it off if you want. I'm going for a shower." He picked out some clean underwear and showered. When he re-entered the room, the TV was off, and Jeanine was under the covers on one side of the bed. He got into the other side of the bed, careful not to disturb her, and clicked off the light.

The memories of the past few hours kept running through his head and wouldn't go away as he lay on his back thinking. What was he turning into? He hadn't even asked himself whether what he'd done to the pastor and the sleaze-ball salesman was right or not. He'd just done it without thinking. Was that because of his Marine training, or was it something inside him?

The look on Payton's face as he lost consciousness swum before his vision, and he groaned aloud.

Jeanine's voice. "You okay there? You're breathing all kind of funny, and you're making weird noises. Don't know if you know you're doing it or not."

"No, I guess I'm not okay," he admitted after thinking about it. "Can't exactly feel proud of what I did this evening."

"Me too." He felt her hand reaching out towards him, and he took it in his. Small, light, dry, warm. It felt nice. That was the best word for it. Nice. "Thanks," he said.

She squeezed his hand gently, and he returned the pressure.

"You want to talk about what happened when

you sent me upstairs?"

"I killed both of them. Double tap."

"Uh?"

"Two shots to the head for each of them."

Silence. "There's something else, isn't there? Something you didn't tell me about when we were in the car."

He groaned. "I don't think I want to tell you."

"Fine." She started to withdraw her hand.

"No, wait. After you'd gone upstairs to the car, the slime-ball was still out cold. Jesus, you must have really hurt him there."

"Hope I did. Wish I'd done the same to Davis."

"I think I hurt him worse before he died."

"Before you killed him, you mean."

"I suppose that's what I mean, yes."

More silence. "Going to tell me about it?"

"Yeah. I got him to put the other guy's — Payton's — dick in his mouth before I shot him."

"You what?" She giggled, and then stopped short. "Jesus, it sounds funny when you say it, but I guess it wasn't funny at the time."

"It wasn't funny for him, for sure. Wasn't funny for me, either, come to that."

"I guess a gun's a great way of making people do what you want them to do. He must have hated it. You should have heard him in the pulpit going on and on about the Sin of Sodom, as he always called it. Maybe he wasn't quite in the same league as those 'God Hates Fags' crowd, but he wasn't that far away from that."

"I can imagine. He seemed like that kind of

self-righteous crap artist. Look, I've got nothing against gays, right? They're a pretty macho bunch of guys in the Corps, but there's some who are gay. Just means they prefer men to women, that's all. If they're good Marines, they're good guys as far as I'm concerned. They're bad Marines, then I have no time for them. What I did to your pastor, I did it because I reckoned it would hurt him more than anything I could do to his body. Nothing to do with what I feel about gays, you understand?"

"I understand. And you actually got him to swallow the other guy's dick? I wish I'd seen it. It must have really hurt his pride to do that."

"Yeah, it did. You should have seen his face when he had to take the guy's dick in his hand, and he knew I was serious about him putting his mouth round it. He took a bit of persuading, but I know ways to persuade people."

"I guess you do at that. You're a horrible man, Henry." But she chuckled as she said it.

"I'm not laughing," he told her, seriously. "Look, I've always thought of myself as one of the good guys. I joined the Corps, did my best for my country, or what I thought was my country." She lay still beside him. "I come back and I find the place has turned to crap. I mean, can you believe it? There's a pastor, for God's sake, sitting there with some real asshole of a con artist, with lines of cocaine in front of them, and they're getting their rocks off watching a movie of kids being raped? I mean, what the fuck has happened here?

What's happened to me?"

"Calm down, Henry. I can feel your pulse racing away, even just holding your hand." Her own hand left his, and moved to his chest, feeling his heart through his undershirt. "Jesus, cool it, big guy. You're going to end up with a stroke or something."

He moved his hand and placed it over hers, pressing it against him. "Thanks, Jeanine. You're good for me, you know."

She leaned over and kissed him on the lips. It took him by surprise, but in an almost reflex action he kissed her back, hard, and wrapped his arm around her body, pulling her closer to him. She was thinner than he had thought she was, and as she rolled over on top of him, she seemed almost weightless. He suddenly realized that he had an erection, and it was pressing against her body through his shorts and her teddy.

She broke the kiss, and remained lying on his body. "Well?" she asked him.

"Well, what?"

"Do you want to?" Somehow one of her hands slipped under his undershirt and started to rub his chest. It felt good – too good for comfort.

"You can feel I want to, can't you? Well, part of me does. You're a pretty sexy woman, you know." And she was, for sure. "But..."

"But what? I want to, you know. You're the first decent man I've met in a long time, it seems to me. You're great with my kids, you've gone way out of your way to help me, you've got a sense of what's right and wrong. And most of the time, you're a great guy to be with."

"Decent? After what I did tonight? I'm nowhere near decent."

"Well, what else could you have done? Call the cops?"

"Yeah."

She laughed. "Reverend Davis is one of those they call Pillars Of The Community, with capital letters all the way down the line. Payton, well, you could see how much money there is there. Porsches and Hummers and big-screen TVs and that sort of shit. And then you come in and say these two are doing coke, and they're watching some evil shit involving kids being tortured for kicks, and they're jerking off to all of this crap. And you've got me tagging along. Unmarried, four kids, just lost her house. Great witness, aren't I? You heard what Davis said, didn't you? I'm emotionally distraught, I can't think straight, whatever. Who are they going to believe? No, you did the right thing, my friend. And I thank you for it." She kissed him again, hard, and rolled off him. "But if you don't want to do it, that's a shame. Because I do, and I can feel that part of you does. Goodnight."

Now he was left with a raging hard-on, and despite all his attempts to think of something else, like the look on Payton's face when Jeanine had squeezed his balls, he kept coming back to Jeanine – the look of her and the feel of her. It wasn't working. Maybe a cold shower or something would help. He started to get up to go to the bathroom.

"What are you doing?"

"Going to the bathroom. Shower."

Her hand reached out and grabbed his arm. "You stupid man. Stay here where you're wanted."There was a rustle of cloth, and he was aware that he was holding her naked body, and it felt good. It had been a long time, too long. Without his being fully aware of it, he was out of his undershirt and shorts, and lying on top of her. Her small tight breasts rubbed against his chest, and he bent his head down and took one in his mouth.

"That feels good," she told him. Her fingers were exploring his back and his buttocks, and he moved rhythmically against her. She clawed at his back, and her breathing became faster and deeper as he continued to press down on her.

"Inside," she said, and with a gasp he entered her. She matched his rhythm and moved back against him, slowly at first, and then faster as he drove them both towards a climax.

He came first, exploding into her, and her orgasm came a few seconds later as she panted and convulsed under him, making low moaning sounds. They lay in an almost stunned silence for a few minutes, and then he rolled off to lie beside her. Both were still gasping for breath.

"You're some man, Henry," she said, when she had recovered her breath.

"And you, Jeanine, are some woman," he told her.

"It's been a long time, hasn't it?" she said.

He nodded, forgetting that she couldn't see him in the darkness, but it didn't seem to matter. She understood somehow.

"Hold me," she said. It wasn't a demand, it was a request, and he was happy to oblige.

They lay there side by side, his arm around her, and her head nestled against his shoulder.

"You smell good. Man smell," she told him.

"Uh-huh. Listen, I know this is way too early to talk about it, but when all this is over…"

She stiffened. "What do you mean? When all this is over?"

"I've got a sister and her kids missing out there somewhere, remember. I want to know what's happening in all this. There's a lot of bad shit happening—"

"Tell me about it."

"—and I want to get to the bottom of it."

"Does that mean you're going to – what was that word you used, 'double tap' – a few more of these guys?"

He thought a moment before replying. "No. Last night was an accident." She giggled nervously. "No, not an accident. But I never planned for that to happen. It was just coming in and seeing those two shitheads sitting there, with that slime showing on the screen…"

"I understand. After all, you saw what I did to Payton."

He winced. "Yes, I did. I'm scared of you, Jeanine."

"And I'm scared of you, Mister Marine, so that makes us quits, right?"

He smiled to himself in the darkness. This was a woman he could live with. It was a long time since he'd felt that way about anyone.

"So what's next on the agenda?" she asked him.

"We go back and we see Allenby."

"If she'll see us."

"She'll see us, don't worry. Maybe she won't want to, but she will."

They drifted in and out of sleep, dozing, waking, finding comfort in each other's presence, making love a couple of times more, before the morning came. And it was really "making love" he thought to himself, not just sex. Strange how you could say that about someone you had only met a couple of days earlier.

Their early breakfast was at a diner near the motel. Jeanine ate a large breakfast, Powers thought that perhaps she was making up for her tiny meals of the day before.

"Yeah, there's that, but sex always gives me an appetite," she explained, before forking in her third hash brown.

"And then we're off to Akron to see Ms. Allenby," he told her.

They drove in near-silence for a few miles, Powers brooding about what had happened the previous evening, and, more pleasantly, what had happened in the motel bedroom. Jeanine's shout broke into his thoughts.

"Stop! Stop the fucking car now. Pull over."

"What?" he said, but did what she asked.

"There was a gray Corolla back there, pulled into the side of the road."

He sighed. "There must be hundreds of gray Corollas out there."

"But you only have one sister, right? You want to find her, don't you?"

"Okay." He got out of the car, and Jeanine joined him as he walked towards the vehicle. "Abandoned," he said, when they could see it a bit closer. "Look, the grass has had time to grow over the tire tracks."

"Doesn't mean that it's not your sister's car, though, does it?"

He looked through the rear window, looking for clues to the owner's identity. He started, and turned to Jeanine, his face bleak.

"Bad news?" she asked him.

"Yes, bad news," he said simply. "I recognize the stuffed toy rabbit on the back seat. I gave it to Holly for her birthday a couple of years back. I picked it out on the Internet when I was overseas, and had it delivered."

"So you never actually saw it?"

"No, but I remember it well. Pink nose and paws, and gray fur and a goofy expression on its face. Definitely the same rabbit."

"Anything else? It might just be a coincidence." She sounded concerned, though.

He looked through the side window. "Holly had a windbreaker just like that one in one of the photos Laroche sent me. And that looks like a T-shirt I've seen on photos of Jason." His shoulders slumped and he his face took on a defeated expression. "You know, I'm not sure I want to see any more. I'm frightened of what I might find."

"That's the first time I've ever seen you look any less than a Marine," she said, leaning against the side of the abandoned Corolla, arms folded, and watching him.

He stiffened and straightened up. "Sorry," he said. He walked around the car, and examined the ground.

"Looking for clues?" she asked.

"Actually, yes. Not that I'm a trained detective, but you never know. You pick up a few things in the Corps. For example, I would say that something heavy was dragged from the car along here." He continued walking along the faint trail, and stopped with a cry of horror.

"What?" Jeanine asked him, moving to join him, but he held up his hand to stop her. "Oh Jesus God and holy fuck," she said, catching sight of the four small bodies and one larger one. She turned away, tears spilling from behind her closed eyelids and her hands clenched in front of her. Powers could half-hear her murmured words, "…blessed Lord Jesus…take them and keep them safe…in your arms for ever…". He said nothing, but remained standing, frozen, staring at the near-naked corpses.

"Dear sweet Lord, look at that. No, don't look," he corrected himself. His knees buckled, and he sank to the ground. "Why? Why? Why?" he moaned to himself. He rocked back and forth, kneeling on the grass, reaching out his hand as if to touch his sister's dead face, and then withdrawing it.

He started at the brush of Jeanine's hand on his arm.

"Come on, Henry. You can't do anything more for them just standing here."

He turned to embrace her, his face glistening with tears. "God, I'm glad you're with me, Jeanine," he said. "I don't know what it would be like if I was on my own. God knows I've seen enough dead bodies in my time. Some of them have been good buddies. But this…" He gestured helplessly at the figures lying motionless in the undergrowth, and buried his face in his hands again. He'd seen his fellow Marines die, and he'd seen villages in Afghanistan populated only by corpses and wailing widows and orphans. But nothing had brought the horror of violent death home to him as this did.

Jeanine kept quiet, waiting, her back turned to the scene of carnage, but watching Powers out of the corner of her eye. At last, he removed his hands from his face.

"We've got to go. There's nothing more you or anyone can do for them here, you know," she told him.

"I suppose you're right." He glanced once more at the remains of his sister and her children, and then stumbled blindly back to the car.

He sat behind the wheel for a good ten minutes, saying nothing, the tears running silently down his face. Jeanine remained silent, but stretched out a hand towards him, touching him lightly on the wrist. He jerked away, and then held her hand, as lightly and as delicately as if it had been an eggshell. Abruptly, he jerked his head up. His voice was steady. "I left them without touching them or saying goodbye to them. The police will want to see them as they are, without me messing things up."

"What happened, Henry?" she asked him softly. I only saw them lying there. I didn't want to look too closely."

"They'd been butchered," he said, bitterly.

"With a knife or something like that. It looked to me as if Laroche had put up some sort of fight to protect the kids. She went down first. Then the kids. Jesus. Bastards." He started to sob again, and then pulled himself up.

"You're allowed to cry, you know," Jeanine told him.

"Sure, but then I'm allowed to get mad, aren't I? I don't know who killed my sister and her children. The police may never find out. Sure, I know enough to be able to tell you what happened – you learn that sort of thing when you've been in enough firefights. I can give you how, but I can't tell you who or why. I can tell you something else, though."

She fed him the line. "What?"

"This whole fucking tragedy would never have happened if Laroche hadn't been kicked out of her house by those bank fuckers. And she'd never have been in that house if she hadn't been sold that crazy fucking mortgage by that crap artist whose dick's now in your pastor's mouth. And he wouldn't have sold her that mortgage if that bitch Allenby hadn't got him to do it. And I'm betting she wouldn't have done that if that little fart Tallman in Columbus hadn't twisted her arm in some way."

"It never ends, does it?"

"And," he went on, as if she hadn't spoken, "I'm willing to bet that Tallman was taking his orders from some shitheel in New York City. Wall Street, to be exact." He seemed to have run out of words for the moment, and sat there, almost panting for breath.

"So what do we do now?"

"First thing is, we go to the police."

She shook her head. "No way, honeybunch."

"What do you mean, 'no way'? We've got a mass murder scene over there. Look, it's my sister and her kids there, but even if it wasn't them, do you think I wouldn't go to the police? Wouldn't you?"

"Henry," she said softly. "Look, don't take this the wrong way, but look at the back of your hand, and look at me. What color are we?"

"So? Should make no difference."

"Should make no difference, sure. Ever heard of being arrested for walking while black?" He shook his head. "Or even losing your life while you're resisting arrest, like my brother did."

"But…" He appeared lost for words.

"This isn't your fucking Marines, Henry, where you're a good Marine or a bad Marine and no-one cares whether you're black, white, brown or even green. I'm guessing Kermit the Frog would fit right in there if he was a good Marine. This is the big wide world out there, Henry." Her voice was still very soft. "They'll want to know exactly what we were up to last night. Are you going to tell them everything we got up to last night? And I'm not talking about what happened in the mo-tel, you understand."

"There's no need for them to know that."

"Oh, they'd want to know. And see how far

you get with 'there's no need for you to know'. Maybe you're a big tough man, and they probably trained you not to crack when the Commies or those naughty Islamic terrorists brainwash you, or whatever the Marines get up to these days, but I'm not that sort of person." Her voice had risen in pitch and volume.

"So we say nothing?"

"No. But we certainly don't go into the police and tell them what we found. It's anonymous tip time, sweetheart. Payphone. One quick sentence telling them where and what, and then into the car and the other side of town as fast as you can make it happen."

He considered this. "I can't believe what you're saying, not on one level, at any rate. But you're not bullshitting me, I know that. So we'll do what you say."

"And we do it from Akron, right, not from out here. You never know. Someone might remember a dark blue Ford out here, stopped outside a payphone. There'll be a working phone at the Greyhound bus station. Park outside somewhere along South Broadway and let me make the call. No-one's going to notice me there. You, you're kind of distinctive, you know. In a good way, mind. Anyway, I reckon you'd probably tell them too much. All that military training, you know."

"And then we just leave them to work the case?"

"Yep. That's what we do. Got a problem with that?"

"I suppose not. Just seems to me that I'm letting Laroche down by not doing more to help."

"And how much fucking help do you think you'd be if you were locked up having the shit kicked out of you?" She sounded angry and she noticed his reaction to her anger. "Listen, Henry, I am truly sorry about what's happened. But it's not. Your. Fault. Okay? And nothing you can do will bring that fine woman and her four lovely kids back to life again. Nothing anyone can do, come to that. You're not a witness or anything. The best you can do is tell the police that it's happened, and let them sort it out. So that's what we're going to do."

"You're right, I suppose. But believe me, I'm going to get even. Not just with your pastor and his friend, or even with that bitch Allenby. This shit goes a long way up, I'm thinking, and I've got a long journey ahead of me. I'm not sure it's a journey I want to take, but since I saw Laroche and her kids, I don't feel I have a choice."

She shrugged. "I don't think I could stop you, even if I wanted to. Your decision, all the way. But we'll make that phone call, okay, and let the police do what they can."

They did what Jeanine had suggested. He parked the car on the street, she made her way to the bus station, and returned a few minutes later.

"That's done," she said, settling herself in the passenger seat and rubbing her hands together.

"What did they say?"

"Never gave them a chance to say anything. Just

the facts, ma'am. So, to the bank?"

He pulled out, and then abruptly took a left.

"Hey! Where are you going? Downtown's the other way."

"I know. I've been thinking."

"Uh-oh. Every time a man says that, it means he's thinking of dumping you."

"Not exactly, but…"

"And that's another one that means the same thing. Been nice knowing you, Henry. Stop the car now, so's I can get out? Pop the trunk, let me get my things? Okay?"

"It's not that." He felt helpless, but he stopped the car. "Just listen a minute, would you? I said I was going to get mad, didn't I?" She nodded. "Well, maybe it's not showing, but I really am mad right now. What I did last night to those two, I'm not proud of what I did, but it had to be done. Same as I don't really like squashing bugs, but you gotta do it sometimes."

"You've told me this."

"And there's more bugs to be squashed."

"By you?"

"By me, like I said. And I don't want you to get mixed up in this, Jeanine. I don't mind them arresting me and throwing me in jail or whatever if they catch me. But you've got kids, Jeanine, and they need you. And…" The words didn't come easily. "I think I'm just that little bit in love with you, Jeanine. Hell, it's more than just what happened last night, but that was great."

"Just a little bit in love? No more than that?"

"I'm not going to make promises I can't keep, and I'm not going to tell you lies, Jeanine. If I come through with all this, I'm going to come after you. I'm going to find you, and then I'm never going to leave you. For as long as you want me."

"Bullshit!" she exploded. "Fucking bullshit, Henry. You used me, and now you're dumping me."

"That's not true!" he protested. "You know it's not true."

"How the hell would I know that?" she asked him. "Now pop the trunk, will you, and let me out."

"Where will you go?"

"Brandi's. Be with the kids."

"And how will you get there?"

"Still got a bit of money from what you gave me yesterday for me and the kids. Greyhound's just down the street, right? No, keep your fucking money," as he reached for his billfold. "I'm not your whore."

"If you want to go to Wilmington, I'll drive you there. No problem."

"I'm not even sure I want to be in the same county as you, let alone the same car, but I'll believe you mean well by that offer." She seemed to calm down a little. "Listen, Henry, I've said you're a good man, and I'll stand by that judgement. Maybe you're not kicking me out after all. Maybe you really don't want to see me mixed up in whatever crazy shit you're going to pull. Fair enough. But don't you come talking to me about how you're going to come after me and love me for the rest of our days until hell freezes over. No, sir. You can take me to Wilmington if you want. But I want you to promise that if you survive whatever it is that you're going to do, you are not, never ever, going to try and find me or have anything to do with me ever again. And you know what I do to the nuts of men who let me down or try to double-cross me."

"I hear you."

"So are you going to take me to Wilmington and kiss me a sweet goodbye for ever?"

"Or?"

"Or am I going to stay with you while you go on your crazy rampage?"

"There's no argument, Jeanine. Your kids are more important. We're off to Wilmington."

"And you promise you're not going to see me ever again, or try to see me?"

"Yes." It hurt like hell, but he had to say it. "It's goodbye at Wilmington."

The drive past Columbus to Wilmington was made in almost total silence. They stopped once for coffee and a bathroom break, and it was almost comical for Henry to see how Jeanine ostentatiously made it clear through her body language that they were most certainly not a couple.

She did kiss him goodbye, though, when he left her at her sister's house. It was a long passionate kiss, and she bestowed it as if she really meant it.

"I'll never forget you, Henry," she told him.

"And I don't mean that shit we did at Payton's. I mean all the other stuff. You singing songs with the kids, buying them pancakes, and all of last night. That was great." She flashed a smile at him and put up a finger to touch his cheek. "But don't, whatever you do, come looking for me again. I couldn't stand that. So it's goodbye, Henry Marine. And the best of luck with whatever it is that you end up doing."

"I hope you won't see my name in the papers," he smiled. "But you might see some things in there and be reminded of me."

"I guess," she said, and smiled. Without warning, she threw her arms around his neck and kissed him again. "You're a beautiful man, Henry. Just too bad. One of those things." She sniffed. "Now just fuck off out of my life before I break down completely."

Powers couldn't see clearly as he turned back onto I-71; the tears in his eyes blurred his vision. He'd given his word to her, though. He wasn't going to see her again. Ever. And that really hurt him.

Sure, he'd been in love before, he told himself as he drove past Columbus. But it hadn't been like this.

TWELVE: AUGUST 2007

He'd originally intended to watch for Allenby as she came into the bank and see which was her car, but the disagreement, if that's what you wanted to call it, with Jeanine, had completely messed up his plans in that regard. It didn't matter. Perhaps he could spot her coming out of the bank when it closed for the evening.

He had to wait until half-past six, trying his best to appear inconspicuous while keeping a watch on the exit that the bank staff were using. The last thing he wanted was an argument with the police or the security guards, so he kept moving around the block, hoping to God that he hadn't missed his quarry.

Damn, it was easier being a Marine, he thought to himself. At least if you were an officer. You could just put your men onto it and order them to stay on watch, taking turns, until they located your prey. And then you all moved in for the kill. This lone hunter thing was a new one for him, and he wasn't sure that he really liked it.

Aha! There she was. Same dinky little gray suit, but a different tie and stuff. Walked as though she had a stick up her ass. And, wouldn't you know it, a red Camaro. Not really what he'd expected, but then he didn't know how much money some-one like her would make at the bank.

Ah well, now he knew where she parked, and what she was driving. He'd be up nice and early the next day to meet her.

He couldn't face the motel where he'd stayed with Jeanine the night before. There were just too many memories, and too much emotional baggage. He found another, which was worse, if anything, but he told himself that he deserved it.

Sleep didn't come easy that night. Images kept floating into his mind. Images of his sister's body, and the bodies of her children. Images of Payton and Pastor Davis. And images of Jeanine, laugh-ing, holding him, making love. And an angry Jeanine, and one kissing him goodbye for the last time. He punched the pillow angrily. He really had fucked up with her, hadn't he? How had he managed to do that? The one woman in years who had made him feel that he could settle down at last, and he had screwed the pooch. Big-time.

His mind wandered into a horrible byway and he felt himself to be trapped in it. What if, he asked, hating himself for even having had the thought, there were lots of kids out there with-out homes, in the same way that Laroche and her children had been, all living in their cars? Easy prey for predators. And what if the predators were not out to kill, but to kidnap those children, and take them away for use in the sort of shit that he'd seen in Payton's house? His stomach heaved, and he rushed into the bathroom and vomited. Surely this couldn't be the case? This was America, right? Things like that didn't happen in the 21st century, did they? Did they?

He rinsed his mouth out with a glass of water, and went back to bed. Had he really saved Jeanine and her three kids from that sort of hell? He guessed it was possible that he had. What had America turned into while he'd been away? Or had it always been like this, and as Jeanine had suggested, the Corps had insulated him from the horrors of most people's everyday lives?

Thinking of Jeanine led to more memories, this time more pleasant, and eventually he managed to catch a few hours of sleep, but it only seemed like a couple of minutes before his cellphone alarm buzzed him awake again.

While he got dressed, he turned on the TV, tuned to the local news station, and the story changed to a report on the gray Corolla and the five bodies found nearby, which had been discovered as the result of an anonymous phone-in the day before. He sat half-dressed on the bed, watching the screen with all his attention focused on the story.

They'd found the murder weapon, a large hunting knife, thrown into the bushes. They'd already lifted prints off it, and they'd matched them to a suspect who was already in custody. Fast work, he thought approvingly.

The screen showed a straggly-haired skinny white guy seemingly in his twenties, with what looked like a serious skin problem. Powers didn't like to typecast people, but "trash" seemed like the best term to describe him.

One that he didn't have to deal with, thank God. The police seemed to have their act together on this. He couldn't remember if Ohio still had the death penalty. He rather hoped not. Life in prison for this shithead would almost certainly be very unpleasant and uncomfortable, while death, even after a long drawn-out appeal process, would be quick and almost comfortable.

Anyway, he had Ms. Allenby to take care of. He finished dressing, and went to yesterday's diner for coffee and eggs. Back in the car, he checked the Colt he'd taken from Payton. It still had five rounds in the clip. Enough to do this job, and the next one on the list.

He checked himself. These were "jobs"? He was talking to himself about taking another human being's life and calling it a "job"? But then, that's what the Marines had taught him to do. Would he feel any different about this if he was wearing the uniform and following orders from those above him? Maybe.

Enough thinking. Time for action. He slipped the heavy pistol into his waistband, and made sure that his windbreaker covered it before driving a block away from the bank's parking lot where he had seen the red Camaro the day before. He got out, leaving the car door unlocked, thinking he would probably need to get out of there quickly, and took up a position from where he could observe the parking lot, without being too conspicuous himself. He spotted the CCTV camera on the pole overhead, and moved out of its angle to avoid being seen.

He didn't have to wait long. He spotted the car as it approached, pulled up the windbreaker's hood to mask his face from the cameras, and moved into a place from where he could approach the driver's door as she backed into her parking slot.

As his shadow blocked the light, she looked up, and saw his tall figure looming over the car. The sun was behind him, and she showed no sign of recognizing him from his previous visit. He'd expected her to shrink back into the car, and perhaps pull out her cellphone and start calling for help, but she surprised him. Looking straight into his eyes, though he was willing to bet that she couldn't actually see his face in any detail, she opened the car door and started to get out, her gaze remaining steadily fixed on him the whole time.

"I'm warning you, boy," she said. "Back off now, unless you want to get hurt. I know what I'm doing here, know what I'm saying?"

Boy? he thought to himself. This really was a triple-dipped bitch he was up against. Made his job even easier.

She was out of the car now, facing him in what looked to him like some kind of martial arts stance. "Now, are you going to move, or are you going to get your ass whupped, nigger?" she asked.

No-one – no white person, at least – had called him that for over twenty years. He reached under the windbreaker and pulled out the Colt.

She laughed. "I'll have that off you before you know what's hit you, boy. And then I'll use it to blow your pecker off." Suddenly, her arm shot out towards his face, followed by a half-spin to deliver a roundhouse kick. Using his Marine training, Powers easily blocked the attempted punch, and swiftly moved sideways, blocking and trapping the kick with his free arm, tucking her foot firmly into the crook of his elbow. She hopped a little on the other leg to maintain her balance, and then stood still. The fight seemed to have been knocked out of her, at least temporarily.

"I guess we look pretty stupid with me holding one of your legs up in the air like this," he said to her. "If I let go of it, are you going to try any more fancy shit like that? I'll grant you, you didn't do badly. You straightened your knee a little too soon on that roundhouse, though. Not good."

She glared at him, and wriggled her leg in an attempt to get it out of his grasp, but he held on to it firmly. "Think you're hot shit, do you? I tell you, boy, if you let go of my leg, I'll be after you again. Better this time. Thanks for the tip, by the way, *sensei*. I won't make that mistake a second time."

"So you're not going to cooperate?"

"Hell no," she laughed. "How long are we going to stay like this?"

"I reckon I can hold your leg for longer than you can stand on the other. My guess is that it's you who's going to collapse first."

"Until another person comes into the parking lot and sees us."

"True," he said. "I'd thought of that, though. Easier for me to shoot you now, right?"

Hate and fear flashed in her eyes. "You wouldn't have the balls to do that."

"Try me," he said, bringing up the gun and squeezing the trigger twice to shoot her in the forehead. He dropped the leg he was holding, cleaned up his brass, and raced for his car parked in the next block.

By the time he heard the noise of the sirens, probably alerted by someone watching the CCTV footage after they'd heard the shots, he was moving, and on his way to I-71. Next stop Columbus.

THE PARKING LOT for employees working at the bank headquarters in Columbus turned out to be under the glass cube, which meant he couldn't repeat his Akron performance with Tallman.

There was no doubt in his mind now that these people deserved what was coming to them. Maybe he wasn't going to humiliate them in the same way that he'd destroyed Payton and Davis, but he had no pity in his heart. Their deaths wouldn't be gentle.

Part of him knew that it was not necessarily these people who were personally responsible for the decisions that had led to his sister and her family, and Jeanine and her family, being kicked out of their houses, but at the same time, he was past caring. Sending a message, that's what he was doing, in the same way that the Marines sent a message when they went after a village in country and wasted it, even though they knew that the vast majority of the villagers who suffered had nothing to do with last week's attacks, for the most part. But then, that was official policy, dictated from way up above. No, this was an OFP – Own Fucking Program.

He was going to have to find another way of doing this one. Even with Harriman, his former corporal, working in security at the bank, it wasn't going to be possible for him to get in to see Tallman in his office. He'd just have to check every damn car as it came up the ramp.

And then, he thought bitterly, the little bastard's probably a tightwad, and he carpools. There's no way that he could just check out the drivers. He looked over to the other side of the plaza. If he could only rent one of those rooms in the building opposite, he thought, looking at the surroundings with the eyes of an experienced infantry officer, he could set up an OP with a pair of field glasses, and stay there for a few days without drawing attention to himself.

Better still, he thought, grinning inside, if there was an unoccupied room in that building that he could just take over without anyone realizing he'd done it, it would leave no trace of his having been there. Not that he considered there would be any real risk of the tenant of an office being associated with the shooting of a banker, but it never hurt to be careful.

He made his way to the building, and studied the list of companies there. The security guard stopped him as he moved towards the elevator bank.

"Excuse me. Sir?" It was barely polite.

"You know me by now, don't you? Meeting with John Carroll at Philip Karshan," picking a firm of lawyers whose name was listed in the lobby. "Same as I did this time last week, and the week before that."

"Sorry, sir." The tone was a little more respectful. "I wasn't here last week, so I didn't recognize you."

He'd deliberately chosen a firm with an office near the top of the building, and he punched the elevator buttons for the 23rd floor, hoping that the guard would notice the indicator. When he reached the 23rd, he quickly located the emergency stairs, and made his way down half a dozen flights before emerging and looking for an unoccupied office or suite. There was one on this floor, but it was on the wrong side of the building.

Down one more flight of stairs. Yes! A "For Rent" sign on a door on the right side of the building, covering the sign of the former tenant, a real estate office. How appropriate, he thought, smiling to himself. Now all he had to do was to see if he could get in. Lockpicking wasn't a skill usually taught by the Marines, but he had picked up a few techniques from one of his platoon who was a genius at it. This had proved a mixed blessing for Lipschitz, as he seemed to be naturally attracted to other people's property, which landed him in trouble, but it had also been a Godsend at times when the platoon was engaged in street fighting and needed to get into a building without employing the usual Marines technique of breaking down the door, which tended to let the world know they were inside.

Amazing what you could do with a thin piece of plastic and a short length of wire, he told himself a couple of minutes later, slipping inside and closing the door behind him. He approached the window, taking care not to be seen from the street. Perfect. With field glasses, it would be easy to see the cars entering and leaving the underground parking space, and their drivers and passengers. Time to get the field glasses, and pick up some ammunition for the Colt at the same time. He went to the door and listened. No-one. He slipped the lock so that he wouldn't have to pick it when he returned, climbed the stairs back to the 23rd floor and took the elevator down to the lobby. The same guard who'd let him in was still on duty, and from the way he was standing, it looked as though he'd been watching the indicators on the bank of elevators. Good, it had been worth the climb, just to make the point that he had never left the 23rd floor.

The guard nodded to him as he left the building. Once in the car, he headed for the outskirts, and in Tuttle Crossing he found a mall with a large sporting goods store. He picked up an expensive pair of field glasses and a small tripod to mount them on, a small backpack, a sleeping bag, a few camping meals which looked like civilian versions of the MREs he'd eaten too many times in the Marines, and a flameless heater for the food, along with a large water canteen. Seemingly almost as an afterthought, he added a carton of .45 ACP ammunition, and paid using cash. Next came a supermarket, where he bought some bottled water and a few bags of snacks, together with a bunch of bananas, all of which went into the backpack.

He decided not to use the front entrance to the office building when he returned, and found his way into a side entrance without much difficulty. It was a long haul with the backpack up to the 16th floor where he was establishing his observation post, but he was in good condition, and made it almost without breaking a sweat.

He set up base camp, mounting the glasses on the tripod, and aiming them at the entrance to the underground parking area. There was an office chair in one corner of the room, and he adjusted it so that he could sit and look through the glasses for long periods without having to strain his back or his neck.

The first cars soon started to make their way up the ramp and out onto the street. He focused the glasses, and was pleased to see how easily the occupants could be identified. He watched until twilight made it impossible to distinguish the occupants of the cars, and decided to give up for the night. Though the hardware store had sold night glasses, he knew from experience that it was almost impossible to identify someone through them. All you could do with them was make out that there was a human being there, and possibly whether it was a man or a woman.

He heated up one of the MREs and wolfed it down. Civilian or military, these things still tasted like shit. The banana was OK, though. He'd missed out on his sleep the night before, so he tidied up the mess from his meal, unrolled the sleeping bag and got into it. He slept fitfully, and was awakened in the early morning by the sun coming through the window onto his face. Time to rise and shine. Banana, and cheese and crackers, washed down with water. He remembered MRE coffee as being terrible. Never mind, he'd make up for it later. But although he watched carefully, Tallman did not seem to be coming to work by car that day, at least at the same time as everyone else.

Somewhat discouraged, he packed away the glasses and tripod, and stowed them in the backpack, which he placed under the desk in the corner of the room before making his way down the stairs to the side entrance of the building. As he stood on the curb, waiting for the crossing lights to change, he suddenly spotted Tallman driving towards the bank. The car screeched to a halt as the crossing lights went green, and he hurried across the road, averting his face. Once across the road, he looked at the car and made a mental note of the silver BMW's license plate as he watched it disappear down the road towards the bank.

Time to call in a possible favor. One of his sergeants had come from Ohio, and had landed a job with the Bureau of Motor Vehicles. Powers wasn't sure whether he would still be working there, but it was worth a try.

Amazingly, when he called, he was put straight through to Enrico Gonzales, former sergeant, USMC.

Gonzales had been one of the best.

"Great to hear from you, sir. I take it you're not calling me at work just to shoot the shit."

"That's right, Enrico. Cut the 'sir', would you? We're both outside now, right?"

"Right. So what can I do for you?"

"Any chance you can give me an address? I give you a name and a license plate?"

"Not me, but I can get it done for you. When do you need it?"

"Today, if you can manage it."

"Hell, I meant five minutes, ten minutes, whatever. We're all fucking keyboard jockeys now, know what I mean? Information at our fucking fingertips."

"No hurry, Enrico."

There was a chuckle from the other end of the line. "That usually meant two minutes in the Corps."

"It means any time in the next hour in the real world."

"Sure. Got a number I can call?"

Powers gave him his cellphone number and the license plate. "It's a silver BMW, couldn't tell you the model number, and the guy's name is Tallman, other names unknown."

"Got it. I'll be back to you within the hour. Semper fi. Sir."

Powers climbed the stairs once again to his OP, turning his cellphone to vibration mode so that he wouldn't be heard when Enrico called back. As it turned out, he got the call within twenty minutes. The address turned out to be a condominium in an upscale suburb of Columbus.

"Thanks, Enrico. One more thing." Powers let his voice slip into Marine officer mode.

"Sir? I mean, yeah?"

"We never had this conversation, OK? I never called you. You never heard the guy's name. If you wrote anything down, my name or number or that license plate, just get rid of it now."

"What the hell are you up to?"

"If I told you, I'd have to kill you." Powers laughed into the phone, but it really wasn't a joke, he told himself. "Seriously, you never heard from me if anyone asks. Semper fi, good buddy."

The line went dead. Powers retrieved his backpack from under the desk, did a quick sweep to make sure he'd left nothing behind, and set off for Tallman's condo building.

FOURTEEN: AUGUST 2007

THE CONDO DEVELOPMENT looked to be pretty up-market, the sort of place that someone driving a BMW would live in. Once again, Powers found himself facing a CCTV camera. The exterior of the condo building, including the entrance to the underground parking, was covered by cameras, and there seemed to be nowhere where he could remain out of their view.

He had a choice. Either inside the building, or outside the grounds, in the road through the landscaped grounds leading to the building. The outside made much more sense. Not only was it less likely that anyone would hear the shots, but he could park the car and get away faster.

He scouted out the lay of the land in the same way that he would have done if he was deploying his platoon. There were some bushes he could use to conceal himself, if he wanted to spring an ambush. Certainly he didn't want to be seen hanging around and chased away or arrested before he had a chance to see Tallman. When he thought about it a little more, he decided it was probably better to wait until the morning and do the job then. He checked the direction with his wrist compass. That spot over there would do nicely. The low morning sun would be shining in his eyes as he turned the bend. Maybe he'd even be adjusting the sun vizor and be distracted. Perfect. Maybe time to find a motel for the night. No, stay in the car, some way away, out in the country, where no-one would come near him. But before that, he needed to eat.

A plate of Applebees ribs later, and he was ready to settle down for the night. He found a secluded spot, set his phone to wake him an hour before sunrise, unrolled his sleeping bag, and re-clined his seat.

Tours in Afghanistan had taught him to be a light sleeper, and the sound of someone moving outside the car instantly brought him to full wakefulness. He reached for the Colt, which he'd loaded with the new ammunition and placed by the sleeping bag before he settled down for the night.

He could make out a dark shape moving around the back of the car, and then a beam of light from a flashlight stabbed into the interior. He quickly hid the hand holding the Colt under the sleeping bag, and feigned sleep as the beam swept over him. The interior of the car went dark again, and he half-opened his eyes. The visitor seemed about to smash open the window on the driver's side.

Operating the door release with one hand, and gripping the pistol in the other, Powers kicked open the driver's door with his feet, still in the sleeping bag. The door caught the intruder under the chin, and he staggered back as Powers freed himself from the sleeping bag's embrace, and leaped out of the car, brandishing the Colt.

"Don't hurt him, mister," came a weak female voice.

Powers ignored this, and stooped to pick up the powerful flashlight that had been dropped by his visitor, who was now lying prone on the grass. A tire iron, which he had presumably been intending to use to break the window, was by his other hand. Powers picked this up and stuck it in his belt. The figure on the grass stirred.

"Up," Powers commanded him. "And you out there, come here too." He shone the flashlight in the general direction from which the voice had come. A waif-like girl, in her late teens, he guessed. Dirty hair, bad skin, torn T-shirt and jeans, and sockless feet stuffed into laceless sneakers. Jesus, he'd seen kids in remote Afghan villages better dressed and groomed than this. He companion started to get up, and froze as he saw Powers and the gun in his hand. The beam of the flashlight fell on his face.

Powers froze motionless in his turn. "Why the hell aren't you in the police station?" he asked. "I saw you on TV the other morning. You'd been taken in for killing——" He stopped short. He wasn't going to insult Laroche's memory by saying her name to this – this thing.

The other got to his feet, and grinned, showing a gappy row of rotting teeth. "Not enough evidence, man. They knew they'd never make it stick, so they just roughed me up a little like they always do, and threw me back on the street. So here I am."

"But you killed them, right?" Powers was smiling, but it wasn't a pleasant smile.

"Sure. The bitch fought back, man. I had to use the knife on her. And then the kids started in, and before I knew it…" He shrugged, still smiling. "Shame about that. Cost me some decent bucks."

"What do you mean?" Powers' smile had become a fixed snarl, but the meth addict didn't seem to have noticed.

"Payton and Davis would pay me a hundred for each of them. Hundred and fifty if they were cute like these were."

What the hell? "Go on." Powers took a step closer, and for the first time the other seemed to fully realize what he was up against. He took an involuntary step backwards.

"I don't know." He hung his head, and Powers could see his jaw clenching and relaxing convulsively.

"I think you do know," Powers told him, and used the tire iron to shatter the intruder's left wrist. He screamed, and his girl moved to help him, but Powers waved the pistol in her direction, and she stayed where she was, obviously terrified.

"You motherfucking bastard," the meth head snarled through gritted teeth. "You cocksucker. What makes you think I want to tell you?"

"Hurts, doesn't it?" said Powers. "Elbows hurt even worse." He moved the tire iron threateningly, and the other shrank back, nursing the broken wrist in the other hand.

"They used the kids." He'd obviously given up any pretence at resistance.

"Used them how?"

"In their movies. You know, man. Home movies. They liked to play these games with the kids. Made videos. You understand, man, special videos. Sold the discs to very special and select customers. They knew there'd be lots of kids out on the road." He paused and moaned. "You fucking asshole," he said to Powers.

"Go on."

"Yeah, right. The way I heard it, the reverend would steer the single moms into a mortgage which Payton would sell them. They'd be out on the street when they couldn't keep up the payments, and then out on the road, yeah..." His voice tailed off.

Jesus, it was as bad as it could get. He regretted nothing about his treatment of Davis and Payton, except that now he had perhaps been a bit too gentle with them.

"What were you doing while all this was going on, sweetheart?" he asked the girl.

"Nothing," she said sullenly, and bit her lip.

"You fucking lying bitch!" said the other. "She

was bait," he explained to Powers. "She stopped in the road and looked pretty, kind of helpless, you know, and the cars would stop. Sometimes they'd open a window or a door and then I could move in and do my thing."

So that's how Laroche had come to be out of the car. He'd wondered about that.

"You asshole!" she screamed at her partner. "You fucking prick! Now he's going to break my arms, isn't he?"

"Wrong, sweetheart," Powers told her.

"You're going to let me go?" she said hopefully.

"No," Powers told her, and fired the Colt. Twice, in the head.

The meth head looked on in horror. "You killed her, you motherfucker. Jesus Christ, she never even saw that coming."

"Death is always unexpected," Powers said to him. "Comes quicker than you think. Except when you really want to die, and then it can't come soon enough." He casually flicked the tire iron against the other's right elbow. There was a thin scream. "Don't think I'm finished yet," he said. He repeated the blow to the same place. Another scream, louder this time.

"You… you… Who the fuck do you think you are anyway, big man?"

"I'll tell you. I'm the brother of the woman in the gray Corolla who you killed the other night. And the uncle of the four little kids you cut nearly to ribbons." His voice was like ice. A cold rage was sweeping through him, and it was all he could do to stop himself beating the other man to a bloody pulp. But this way would hurt the murderer more. The demon of revenge was carrying him into unknown dark corners of his soul, and part of him was sickened by what he saw himself doing now.

Absolute terror in the other's face. "Oh holy shit. I guess I really fucked up, didn't I?" Powers nodded silently. "What the hell are you going to do to me now? Take me back to the police?"

Powers shook his head. "I could hurt you a lot more," he said, reflectively. "Break all your fingers, for a start. That hurts a lot. Kneecaps are pretty painful, too. But I guess you're in enough pain right now." There was an anguished nod in reply. Tears had started to run down the addict's face. "Hurts, does it?" Another nod. "Good. Then I'll sit here in the car, and you can stand out there. On one leg. Go on, lift up one leg. Don't try and run away or put your leg down. If you do, I won't shoot to kill, know what I mean? When you get tired of standing out there, you can let me know, and we'll see if it's time for you to stop standing."

It took a little time for all of this to sink into the other's understanding. "You're the devil himself," he half-whispered, hoarsely.

"No, son, I think you're confusing me with your former employers. Now if you'll excuse me, I'm going to make myself comfortable." He returned to the car, and sat, the door open, facing the moaning would-be robber.

"I need to take a dump," complained the meth

head after a while, hopping about as he tried to keep his balance.

"Do it in your pants," commanded Powers.

"No fucking way, man. That's disgusting."

"Disgusting?" laughed Powers bitterly. "I bet I can make you crap your pants." He rose, and ostentatiously racked the slide of the Colt before putting it to the other's temple. A foul smell filled the air, and the meth head shivered. "See? Told you I could make you shit yourself." He returned to the car.

"I think I want you to..." But he couldn't bring himself to beg Powers to put him out of the pain and humiliation he was experiencing.

"I can wait," said Powers.

Another thirty agonizing minutes. "You motherfucking prick. I can't take it any more. Just get it over with, will ya?"

"My pleasure," said Powers, and fired two shots.

HE PICKED UP THE SHELL CASES, left the bodies, and drove away from the scene. Along the way to Tallman's condo, he tossed the brass into the bushes, leaving half a mile or two between each case. He felt a little sick at what he'd just done, but the sense of relief that he'd avenged Laroche and the kids was almost sexual in its intensity.

He parked the car a little less than a mile away from Tallman's house and made his way to the hiding place he'd noted the previous day. He'd changed his plans.

The cars started to leave the condo, and Powers, crouched behind the bushes, watched anxiously for the silver BMW. Ah, there it was. He quickly used the field glasses to check the license plate, and swore to himself.

Tallman was driving, but there were two small children in the back. Obviously it was Tallman's job to take the kids to school that day. He could wait till the evening and trust that Tallman wasn't collecting them from school, or even wait until the next day and hope that Tallman wouldn't have the children with him then. But then the memory of Laroche and her children rose to the surface. His beloved kid sister and her four lovely kids, who would never have died in that obscene way, killed by the scum whose bodies were now lying in the undergrowth some five miles away, if Tallman had not been selling these fake mortgages to Wall Street and buying himself a BMW with the proceeds.

The memory propelled him into the driveway in the path of the BMW, waving the Colt. For a moment, it looked as though Tallman intended to keep driving and knock him down, but Powers fired the gun once, at the offside front wheel. He missed, but the bullet ricocheted off the roadway, and pinged the body of the car. Seemingly shocked, Tallman brought the car to a halt, and took his hands from the wheel, raising them in the air.

Keeping his face turned away as much as possible, Powers motioned to Tallman to open the passenger door, waving the gun to emphasize his point. He heard the click of the lock, and jumped inside, keeping the gun trained on the banker, who was obviously terrified. There was no sound from the children in the back.

"First right and second left after that," he told Tallman, giving directions that would take them towards the place where he had left his car. His face was partly averted, and half-hidden by the windbreaker hood. He didn't want Tallman to recognize him.

"And if I don't?" asked Tallman, with what looked to be his last reserve of bravado.

Powers said nothing, but merely prodded the muzzle of the pistol into Tallman's ribs.

"Okay, I get your point. But you leave my kids alone, right?"

Silence from Powers. They took the first right and the second left. "Stop here," said Powers. "Turn off the engine. Give me the keys. Open the back door. Let the kids out. Tell them to walk back the way we came and go back home."

Tallman started to protest, but a jab in the side with the Colt changed his mind, and he carried out the orders. The children started to protest, but Tallman ordered them out, and they started walking.

Powers kept watching them in the driving mirror as they made their way down the road. When they had turned the corner, he turned to face Tallman, who was now seeing his face clearly for the first time, and let out a gasp.

"I thought I recognized the voice. What more do you want from me? I can't help you or your sister, you know."

"Correct. She's dead, and it's all your fault and the fault of your fucking bank."

"She took on something she couldn't keep up with. We had every right in the world to repossess the house. We were under pressure to sell those subprime mortgages."

"Subprime?" It was not the first time that Powers had heard the word. Payton had used it. "What does that mean?"

Tallman was almost laughing. "Never heard the word before? Where have you been?"

"Afghanistan," Powers said. He felt stupid for not keeping up with the news, but unlike some of his fellow Marines, he hadn't spent all his off-duty time glued to the CNN channel or Internet news sites. He'd taken his duties to the Corps seriously.

Tallinn's face changed a little. "Subprime is the word we use to describe loans made to people whom we wouldn't usually consider a good risk. Their credit rating is below prime."

"So why make loans you know that you're not going to get the money back on?"

"We were being forced by the pols in Washington to make loans to minorities. That includes people like your sister."

"You? Your bank? Forced?"

"Well, perhaps not forced. Strongly encouraged, perhaps. And not just us, of course, but all banks all over the country. The idea was to turn America into a nation of homeowners."

"Don't you guys have some sort of checks on people before you lend them money?"

Tallman smiled a thin smile. "Yeah, but we ignored them. For instance, one of the suckers would tell us they earned fifteen thousand a year. We'd write down seventy-five. Or they had a couple of hundred in the bank. We'd add a few zeroes at the end. And we'd lend them more than the property was worth. Let them buy some nice things for the place. Then they could flip the place."

"Flip?"

"Jeez, you really have been away, haven't you? They'd sell the house for more than they paid for it and borrow a bit more to go upmarket."

"That assumes that the price of property is always going to go up."

"Right. Which it always did."

"But no more? What a clever little scheme you had going, didn't you?" Powers' voice was almost silken, caressing. "And then you could sell all these bad loans off to Wall Street, and you could make money, they were nothing to do with you any more, and it wasn't your problem? That sounds like a really smart way of doing business. You must be a pretty good businessman." Tallman nodded. He seemed to be basking in the compliments. Powers' tone suddenly changed to a low snarl. "You may think you're a good businessman, but I'm telling you that you're a lousy shitty human being. An asshole."

Tallman cringed in his seat. "I can't get your sister's mortgage back," he whimpered.

"No, you can't, and you can't bring my sister back. Because, asshole, some lowlife fuck killed her and her four kids. Because she was out on the street in her car, as a result of you being such a good fucking businessman, asshole."

"It wasn't my fault, was it, if she didn't want to

go into a shelter?"

"I'm sure she had her reasons for staying out of a shelter. She wasn't dumb, you know. That seems to be the problem with you people. You seem to think that because some people don't have money, they don't have brains. You know what? I think it's the other way round. It's the rich people who don't have brains. They pay other people like lawyers and accountants to do their thinking for them. The poor people have to do their own thinking, and they get good at it. They get smart. Take me, for example. I'm not exactly poor, but I'm a long way off being rich. And I've been doing a lot of thinking lately, and I've come to a conclusion."

"What?"Tallman licked his lips nervously.

"You're going to die. Some time in the next five minutes."

"You can't do that!"

"Why?"

"The police will catch up with you."

"So? Maybe they will, maybe they won't. They haven't caught me yet and there's five bodies lying around that I'm responsible for, so far, that is. Maybe you will increase the odds of them catching up with me. But before we say goodbye, maybe you can give me some advice?"

"Why should I? What do I get out of it?"

"The chance to die quickly and painlessly rather than slowly in agony. But it's your choice. You don't have to help me if you don't feel like it."

Tallman swallowed. "What do you want to

know?"

"Who you sold the mortgages to in Wall Street."

"All of the big names."

"You giving me the name of any people there?"

"Not off the top of my head. Even if I could, they've probably moved on. They don't stay in one place for long, these people." He looked fearfully at the gun in Powers' hand. "What's going to happen to my kids if you kill me? Thought of that?"

"They have a mother?" Tallman nodded. "She's a good mother?"

"The best."

"She'll find another man, then, and the kids will have a new father, and they'll grow up and forget all about you. In just the way that my sister's kids will never grow up now, thanks to you and your buddies in the bank and on Wall Street." Tallman put his hands over his eyes. "Don't like to think about it? Don't blame you, really. Not very nice when it comes down to it, is it? But I'm being nice. Rather than killing your kids and letting you spend the rest of your life without them, you're going to go nice and quick, and they're young. They'll get over it soon enough."

"You're a complete prick, you know that, don't you?" This was said in a completely flat and neutral tone. There seemed to be no resistance left in the man.

"No, that's you. Maybe I'm not that nice a person, but I think you're the prick. So, I don't know if you believe in anything up there, but if you do, I'll give you a minute to say your prayers or make your peace or whatever."

There was no point in making the man suffer more than he had to, Powers said to himself. At the end of the minute, he raised the gun. "Open the driver's door would you? No, stay where you are, in the driver's seat. I just don't want to break the window with the bullets. Thank you." He fired twice, and Tallman fell forward, his blood dripping over the steering column. Powers picked up the two shell cases, and wrapped his hand in a handkerchief before opening the passenger door, getting out and shutting it, using the handkerchief to wipe any possible prints off it.. He also closed the driver's door, and wiped that as well before setting off for his hire car.

He drove to the airport, returned the car, and bought himself a ticket to New York. He wasn't sure what he was going to do there, but he was certain that he would find his way in the big city.

POWERS WAS UNFAMILIAR with New York. If he was honest with himself, the city frightened him with its noise and its crowds, and he felt himself swamped by the sheer weight of numbers. He'd grown up in a small town, and he'd spent too long in the remote parts of the world for a city to be comfortable. He'd found himself a small studio apartment, and started counting his money.

At the rate he was spending, he was going to have to find himself a job. Security guard seemed to be what he thought he could manage without too much trouble. He had a horror of being stuck behind a desk from nine to five, and the alternatives seemed to be warehouse work or other manual labor, which he was prepared to do if nothing better came along, but it wasn't his first choice. He went to several companies hiring security guards, but when he told them of his rank in the Marines, they laughed in his face.

"There's no way we could take you on as a

guard," they told him. "I'm sure you could do the job, but hell, a major coming in and doing that work? You'd be bored out of your skull after the first hour."

One agency, sponsored by a part of the VA program, was more constructive. The interviewer was also from Ohio, and Powers discovered that they had a few contacts and acquaintances in common. At least it meant that Powers wasn't thrown out of the room after the first few minutes, which is what most of the others had done, and his experience as a Marines officer counted for a lot.

"I can't promise you regular work," said the interviewer, "as you're too highly qualified for the usual posts, but it seems to me that you'd be perfect for some things that we handle."

"Such as?"

"We need some people with social skills and brains as well as muscle. We're not your usual type of company in this game, and we handle quite a few VIP gatherings and the like, given that we only employ vets. You wouldn't wear a uniform, but you'd be keeping an eye on things, and you'd be in charge of a team of about a dozen people. We don't get a lot of these events, but when we do they pay well, and so do we. Interested?"

It sounded a lot better than most of the jobs he'd been looking at so far, and he accepted the offer.

The whole business turned out to be more

interesting than he had imagined. When he first met the team of guards he was meant to be leading some days before the event took place, he was horrified.

He stormed into the office, and slammed his fist down on the table.

"Are you trying to insult me?" he demanded.

"How's that?"

"The mob you've given me for the reception next Thursday. What the hell am I meant to do with them? Two of them are out of their heads on something – I don't know what, and I don't want to know. One doesn't seem to have enough sense to be able to tell his left from his right, and the other three look as though they've just come off the streets where they've been living rough."

"They have," said his boss.

"How do you mean?"

"These are basically good guys, Henry. They all had good jobs and all lost them through no fault of their own. They've been living rough for some time now. Our organization, if I have to remind you, is trying to give a helping hand to these people and others like them. We want you, and people like you, to give them some pride in what they're doing. I've looked at your service record, Henry. I've got faith that you can turn these guys round and help them stand tall. Yeah, it's a challenge, but I think it's one you can meet."

"You sound like my colonel," grinned Powers.

"Don't be too Marine-style rough on them, though. These guys have been through a lot.

Build them up. Give them some self-respect."

"I'll do what I can," Powers told him, though he had a feeling it was going to be a hopeless task.

It turned out better than he expected. Once they realized that he was basically on their side, they almost all responded, including the ones he had written off as hopeless. He was able to restore the self-respect and pride to a scruffy bunch of derelicts, and get them functioning as a team.

"It's the first time since I left the Army that anyone's bothered to talk to me as if I was a human being with some intelligence, and not some animal," one of them said to him as he instructed them on the way to check guests' credentials, how to escort a drunk VIP out of the way where he could do no further damage to himself or to others, and all the other little tricks of the trade that he had been given in a manual presented to him by the management.

By the time the big evening arrived, his team was ready, and they performed their duties without a hitch, looking dapper in their hired tuxes.

The next morning, the manager called him in. "You've done better than we expected with that crowd. We may write the manual and tell you what to do, but it's guys like you – and there aren't too many of you – who can make it actually happen. You and your squad are going to be the A-Team for this sort of event in the future. There's a big Wall Street event next week we'll put you on. One of the banks is doing a presentation for investors, and needs security. You're it."

Powers had been wondering how he was going to find out more about the way that the Wall Street banks had been working. This seemed to be his chance.

HE STRUCK LUCKY — luckier than he had ever imagined would be possible. On the night of the event, a senior vice-president of the bank seemed to be drinking his champagne and laughing quite happily with his colleagues and clients. The next minute, he was lying flat on his back, red-faced and gasping for breath. The smartly dressed men and women surrounding him seemed to freeze in horror, with apparently no idea what they should be doing.

Powers swooped in and took in the situation at a glance. He'd seen heart attacks before, and this wasn't a heart attack. Using all his strength, he seized the portly banker, and dragged him semi-upright before performing the Heimlich maneuver. A chunk of half-chewed lobster canapé shot out of the man's mouth, hitting the silk gown of one of his female companions, who moved away in some disgust. The man started to breathe heavily and raucously, and stared at Powers, his eyes gaping.

"You ... saved ... my ... life," he managed to gasp out. He half-sat, propped up on his elbows, and looked at Powers a little more closely. "Thank you. Who are you, anyway?"

"I'm in charge of the security detail tonight, sir."

"Well you did a hell of a job. Thank you isn't enough. What's your name?"

"Powers, sir. Henry Powers."

"One hell of a job there, Henry." He put out a hand, and Henry grasped it. "Army?"

"Marines, sir. Major."

"I'm impressed. They taught you well, Major Powers."

THE NEXT DAY, Powers reported to work, and was immediately called to see the manager.

"I've just had a call from the Swiss bank who hosted the reception where you worked last night. It's fine. Nothing wrong. Don't look so worried, Henry. You saved a guy's life?"

"I guess I did. He was choking, and I applied the Heimlich maneuver. It worked. He thanked me."

"Look at this." He thrust a tabloid newspaper in Powers' face. There was a photo of Powers with the stricken banker, fighting to apply the Heimlich maneuver.

"Where the hell did that come from? I didn't see any reporters there."

"I'm guessing one of the guests there must have taken a picture with their phone. It certainly doesn't look like a professional picture, does it?"

"Stupid assholes," remarked Powers. "Taking pictures and doing fuck all."

"I've been fighting off the reporters and the TV stations this morning. Told them there were no interviews or anything like that until you say it's okay."

"It's not okay." Powers was sullen.

"I thought you'd say that. Well, as a result of all of this, you're not working here any longer."

"What?" Powers was stunned. "Because I don't want to talk to the press?"

"No, nothing like that. Don't worry. You've got a better job. This guy whose life you saved has suggested you join his bank as deputy chief of security. He called me an hour ago and asked what sort of guy you were. I told him, and he wants to see you this morning. I tell you, Henry, the job is yours if you want it, and I am sure it will pay a lot better than we've been paying you. And if you don't want to take it, for whatever reason, I'll be more than happy to have you continue working here."

"Well…" Powers was taken aback. "I was only doing my job. He wants to see me? What should I wear?"

"You sound like a high-school girl worrying about her prom date. What you're wearing now. Get your ass over there."

"Where's 'there'?"

The manager slipped him a card. "This is the place you go to, and you ask for a Carl Reichman.

He's the guy whose life you saved last night."

The Swiss bank appeared modest by comparison with the bank in Columbus, but when Powers looked closer, it was much more classy. What had been laminate or veneer in the Ohio bank seemed like solid hardwood here, and the fittings, rather than being shiny chrome, were brushed stainless steel. He guessed this is what they meant when they talked about European style, or maybe it was New York rather than Europe in this case.

He felt sadly out of place in the lobby, waiting beside two dudes in their Wall Street suits with their scrubbed pink faces and shining shoes. Life in the Marines hadn't taught Powers much about men's clothes, but even he could tell that these looked like expensive threads.

He twisted his hands uncomfortably in his lap as he waited for Reichman, who had said that he wanted to meet him, but didn't look as though he was going to show up.

Reichman arrived in the lobby some twenty minutes after he had made the appointment. The two suit dudes had met their appointed representative long ago and had left. He didn't bother to apologize, but came straight up to Powers, and wrung his hand. "Great to see you, guy," he said. Powers could detect a faint trace of a European accent. "Eaten yet?" He looked Powers up and down. "Come on, they'll let you in if you're with me."

Powers had hardly ever felt so embarrassed.

At the place he was taken, it looked as though the price of a drink of mineral water, which is what everyone seemed to be drinking with their lunch, would eat up a month's wages. And everyone seemed to be eating raw fish with chopsticks. Powers had never got the hang of chopsticks, despite spending a few months in Okinawa.

"What will you have to drink?" Reichman asked him, when they had been shown to a table in the back of the restaurant.

"Uh… just water is fine," Powers answered. Was this a job interview? If so, it was probably not a good idea to drink any alcohol, though he could certainly use a cold one.

"Sure? The Pouilly-Fumé is good here. Goes great with the sushi. We'll split a bottle."

What the hell was he talking about? "Sure."

It turned out to be a rather dry white wine. Reichman raised his glass in Powers' direction. "Here's to you, sir," he toasted. "If it wasn't for you, I doubt if I'd be here today. Those other assholes didn't seem to have any idea what to do."

Powers mumbled something about its only being his job, and it was nothing. If he had still been in the Corps, he would have known how to handle the situation, but being in civilian clothes, with no obvious rank system, still bothered him a lot.

"Cheers," he said, raising his glass in reply.

"And what to eat?"

"I've no idea." Powers managed a smile. "I think you'd better order for me."

"Any allergies? Anything you can't eat? Sea-urchin, for instance?"

Sea-urchin? Wasn't that the spiny thing that poisoned you if you trod on it, or something? How the hell would you begin to eat something like that? "I guess I can try it. Never eaten it."

"It's good here." Reichman called over a waiter and ordered. Powers didn't know what the hell he was talking to the waiter about. "So," Reichman said, when he had finished displaying his knowledge of the menu, and turned back to face Powers, "I guess you may be wondering why I asked you here."

"They said something about a job, but I don't think I caught all of the details."

"Yep, it's a job. Deputy head of security with us. It's a pretty responsible job., you understand? We have nearly a thousand people working for us here in New York. And I don't need to tell you that we're all pretty worried about what might happen in the future. All those crazies coming over, right? You've been over there, and I admire that. All of you guys are doing a great job keeping us safe here. So I guess you understand those people pretty well, huh?" He spoke rapidly in short sentences, obviously not expecting an answer, but paused to suck in more wine from his glass.

"Who would I be reporting to? And what powers would I have?"

"You like to know these things? Good for you. Quite right. In theory, I guess you'd report to Bill

Marshall, but he's an asshole. Yeah, you'd probably report to Sam."

"Sam?"

"Sam Ogilvy. CEO of the bank here in the USA. Know much about computers?"

"Er, not really."

"That's okay. No problem. Bill's into them, and doesn't seem to be bothered about the little things like keeping the bad guys out. Would you believe we had some nutcase asshole waving a gun at our receptionists last week? They called the cops, and they took him away. But if they'd been slower, or he'd been quicker... I don't even want to think about it."

"What was all that about?"

The waiter arrived with two plates of sushi. Powers picked up his chopsticks and immediately dropped one on the floor. He requested a fork, somewhat to the waiter's silent contempt. Fuck him.

"Yeah, he was complaining that we'd taken his house away from him."

Powers sat up straight inside, but tried not to let anything show. "How do you mean? You don't do mortgages, do you? I mean, I don't know a lot about the banking business, but it seems to me that you guys are too big for that sort of thing."

"Yeah. Well, what we do, we buy the mortgages off the thrifts and the small banks out in the country, and we package them up and trade them as bonds. That's my job. I'm the chief ABS trader. And though I say it myself, Henry, I'm pretty fucking good at it."

"ABS?"

"Asset Backed Securities. Fancy name for a load of mortgages all stuck together and sold on. Pile of shit for the most part, but there's a lot of people out there want to buy them. And it's my job to make them want to buy them."

Powers shook his head in simulated wonder. "Well, I live and learn. And you trade these things?"

"Yep. I whip 'em and drive 'em."

"I'd heard a lot of mortgages these days are going to folks who don't deserve them," Powers offered.

The other shook his head and shoveled in a lump of raw tuna on rice. "Not my problem, Henry. Not our problem. Those stupid assholes want to buy houses they can't afford, am I going to stop them? No way. Keep 'em coming. The more the better."

"Are all the mortgages real? I mean, are they really mortgages?"

"Come on, Henry. It's all money. What's real, what's not? More wine? Who cares?"

"Thanks. So how do you know how these mortgages are really worth?"

"The rating agencies look at them and put a stamp on them. Sort of seal of approval."

Henry was thinking furiously. The sushi was probably the best in New York — it was at least the most expensive meal he had ever eaten in his life — he'd seen the prices on the menu — but it was turning to ashes in his mouth. But at the same time, he had a sense of fulfillment. Almost without trying, he'd come face to face with one of the men who was responsible, somewhere down the road, for his sister's death and the deaths of her children. And he'd saved the asshole's life.

"Tell me more about the job," he asked.

"Well, it's not me who's got the details," Reichman smiled. "But basically, let Bill handle the IT security side of things, and you look after the physical side. Make sure the security gates are working, people's card access is all OK. The right people are where they're meant to be, and the peasants are kept out. That sort of thing. I bet you could do that sort of thing blindfold."

"You can offer me that job? I thought you said you were a trader?"

"I am. I'm the best fucking trader they have. You saved my life last night, right? No, wait," holding up a hand. "You did. None of those other assholes would have done a thing. So they owe you, and they'll do what I tell them to do. You on board?"

"I guess so." Powers deliberately made his voice hesitant, though he was shaking with excitement inside. This was his chance to find out all about the world that had killed his sister and her children. Right at the top. "What's the money?"

"As much as you want, within reason. How does a hundred twenty sound to you? Maybe it doesn't sound like a lot, but with the bonus, of course, it could end up topping the two fifty mark."

"Sorry?"

"A hundred and twenty thou a year."

"Oh." It was a lot. A lot more than he had been earning in the Marines, even with all the goodies and extras. "Sounds fine," he said, keeping his voice as calm as he could.

"Then that's settled. Great. Cheers." He refilled their glasses, emptying the bottle. "We'll get you signed up when we've drunk this. Cheers."

"Cheers."

Thanks to Reichman's bullying tactics with the HR department, and the publicity that Powers had received for saving his life, the employment process took almost no time at all. Since he'd served in the Marines as a commissioned officer, they told him he could start work the next day, even though it usually took time for a background check.

"What do you expect me to wear to work?" he asked, somewhat intimidated by the clearly expensive clothes surrounding him, and looking down in some embarrassment at his windbreaker and jeans.

"Good point," said Reichman. "I guess you should wear a suit. Got one you can wear into here?"

Henry shook his head. It just wasn't one of those things you needed in the Corps. The last time he'd worn a suit must have been at his high school prom. He shook his head at the wonder of it all.

"Then you buy yourself one," Reichman told him, peeling off half a dozen hundreds from a roll. "Forget it. You don't need to pay me back. You saved my life, remember?"

This was going to be a different world, Powers thought to himself, as he folded the bills and put them carefully in his pocket. He reckoned you could dress pretty sharp with six hundred dollars.

A FEW WEEKS LATER, Powers was just leaving the bank after a long day. All the days were long, and the work was surprisingly tough, though nothing like as hard as leading a platoon of men through the Afghan mountains. He was earning his money, for sure, though.

It felt good to be dressed right. He'd obviously hit the right mark, not too sober and not too flashy, and his tie was straight out of the fashion plates. His nominal boss, Bill, was more interested in the computers than the nuts and bolts of physical security, as he had been warned, and tended to dress like a nerd. As a result, the senior management, impressed by how Powers had immediately taken to the job, made sure that he was the point man for all visitors, rather than his superior, and he'd soon become "Henry" again, which hadn't happened to him in a long time, after being addressed by his rank and last name for so many years.

It felt good to be trusted and secure. Reichman had continued to be friendly, but it was hard to reconcile the jovial back-slapping trader with the man who was, Powers was ever more convinced, one of the main movers behind the whole sub-prime mess.

Reichman had introduced Powers to his counterpart in another bank, Charles Sanfion, and they'd gone out to an expensive bar one evening, where they'd sunk the best part of two bottles of Finnish vodka between the three of them while Reichman and Sanfion discussed what seemed to be the finer points of mortgage trading, which sounded more like physical assault than business dealings.

"…rip his fucking face off…"

"…let him have it in the nuts and then go for the jugular…"

"…stamp on the little fucker till he bleeds…"

Naturally, Powers had nothing to add to this conversation, but it became clear to him that these two men were quite possibly the most important men on Wall Street in the mortgage business, even allowing for the massive egos they displayed, which made the average Marine look like a modest retiring virgin. There were also things called "rating agencies", it learned, which put a seal of approval on the bonds that the "grunts" in the back office put together from the crappy mortgages before the traders sold them off to the suckers who would buy them – small German banks, large Japanese banks, pension funds, whoever. Powers' blood had boiled, but the Corps had taught him to hide his emotions, and he had sipped his overpriced vodka calmly, pouring most of it into a potted plant when the others weren't looking. He had refused the lines of cocaine that were offered, pointing out that he was, after all, the deputy head of security at the bank, a fact which Reichman seemed to find extremely amusing.

Stepping out of the bank onto the street, and turning towards the subway entrance, he thought he heard his name being called. He turned, and to his amazement saw Jeanine running towards him.

Without thinking, he held out his arms, and she rushed into them. "What? Why? How?" was all he could say, as he felt her body pressed against him.

She disengaged herself from his embrace, and looked up at him. "My, haven't you gone up in the world, Henry?" she said. "You're a pretty cool dude, you know?"

"Yeah," he said, embarrassed. "But how…?"

"You were famous for a while, you know. You saved that rich guy's life, and you were in the paper, and that got onto the Internet, you know that? I looked at the picture, and I thought to myself, 'Well that guy's wearing a tux, and the guy I knew never wore a tux, but he sure as hell looked like the guy in the photo."

"Yeah?"

"Yeah. And I did a little bit of phoning around. Found out a bit more about the event. Guessed you'd been doing security. Bit more phoning. Gave that vet agency your name, and told them I was your cousin. And here I am, Mr. Clean Marine. Though you sure as hell don't look like a Marine dressed up like that."

"Smart work on your part. Where are the kids?" He had to think about their names. "Lisa, Tyrone and Kareema?"

"With their aunt Brandi."

"So you came here to see me?" She nodded. "After telling me you never wanted to see me again?" She nodded again. "Where are you staying?"

"Only arrived here this morning. Found this bank and waited in the coffee shop opposite till I saw you come out."

He shook his head. "You could have called the bank and asked to speak to me."

She smiled. "Henry, I don't even know your fucking name, you know that?"

"And I don't know yours." He smiled back. "We're a really strange couple, aren't we? Where's your bags?"

"One bag. The coffee shop said they'd look after it while I looked for you."

They picked up the bag, and he swung it easily onto his shoulders as they took the subway to the small apartment he'd rented after starting work with the bank.

"Nice," she said, standing in the doorway with her hands on her hips and looking around. "This must cost."

"I get paid enough," he said.

"Yeah, nice."

He changed into a T-shirt and jeans and came out to find her seated on the couch, drinking a beer that she'd found in the fridge, and looking through a book on financial derivatives.

"Do you really understand this shit, Henry?"

"I'm trying, but no. I'm not dumb, but this takes a special form of smart, I reckon. Not my kind of smart, anyway. You hungry?"

"Sure."

"We can send out for something. What do you want? Vietnamese?"

"Sure. Whatever. Come here, you stupid man." She almost attacked him, tearing off his T-shirt, and fumbling with his jeans. He was only a little less gentle in removing her clothes, and their bodies joined together fiercely. He gasped with sheer pleasure as he entered her, and she twisted and flexed her way under him to reach her climax.

"Jesus," she said, panting, when he came, and he moved off her. "That was good. I've been dreaming about that since I said goodbye to you at Brandi's." She looked at him with a critical eye. "You're a fine man, Mr. Henry Marine. Now you can send out. I'm hungry. Where's the shower?" He showed her the bathroom, found her a clean towel, and left her to shower while he ordered the food. She emerged, and he took his turn in the shower.

The food arrived, and they ate in near silence.

After they had eaten, he fetched two beers from the fridge, and she lay back, cradled against his chest.

"So how are you getting on against the mortgage bastards?" she asked him. "No-one dead yet?"

"It's not a joke, Jeanine," he told her. "I'm serious about this, you know. I'm not going to go onto the trading floor and wipe out a whole lot of people on the off-chance one or two of them might be the bastard who sold on your mortgage, or sold on Laroche's mortgage. We did enough of that in Afghanistan, and it made me feel sick. I wanted the biggest and baddest of them all, and I found him, Godammit." He started to laugh.

"What's so funny?"

"He's the guy whose life I saved. He's the one who's the biggest and baddest of them all playing these crazy games with other people's money. So he gives me this job that I've got now to say thank you, and then I find out he's the guy I came to New York for. Funny?"

She didn't laugh. "The word you want is 'irony', Henry. So have you made up your mind what you're going to do?"

He nodded. "I made up my mind today. Before I met you this evening, I was going to wait outside his house tomorrow morning, wait till he got in his car, and then stop his car and shoot him there."

"Make it look like a robbery?"

"Actually, no. I wasn't going to take anything.

Rather, I was going to leave him with thirty bucks."

"Uh?"

"Think about it."

She thought. "Oh, right. You go right ahead with your plans, Mister Marine. I'll be here waiting for you. And I'll make sure that someone hears me with you all the time you're gone."

"How do you mean?"

"I'm going to give you the best alibi you could ever want. They're going to be banging on the door to get you to stop screwing my brains out when I start making the right noises."

He laughed. "That's great, Jeanine. You know what will happen to us if we get caught, don't you? They may not give a damn about the pastor and his friend, but they sure as hell are going to mind me doing a double-tap on a Wall Street banker, and you'll be in the shit with me, you know."

"Then they'd better not catch us, had they?" she said. "What time were you going to start?"

"I'd be up at four in the morning. He starts work early to tie in with the overseas markets."

"Then we'd better get some sleep."

"You think I can sleep with you beside me?" he grinned.

"You gotta try. And then you think you can go to work and do your job?"

"Sure." He shrugged.

"You're one cool dude, Mister. Let's hit the sack."

He left at four the next morning and came back a little after six.

"Done?"

He nodded. "Done. How was the alibi?"

She grinned at him. "Great. According to one of your neighbors, you're a sex-crazed maniac, you know that, and I'm nothing but a goddamned whore."

"Well done. Now to get out of these street clothes, shower, and put on the snappy threads. Busy day today."

"How so?"

"Some asshole just shot one of our traders. Reckon the bank's deputy security chief is going to get involved with this business somehow."

The black humor of the situation hit her, and she started to giggle. "That's so fucking funny it's not funny," she said. "You're going to have to investigate yourself. That is, like, so screwy it's untrue. Will you be able to stop laughing?"

"If I want to stay out of prison, I'm going to have to, aren't I?" He came out of the bathroom about ten minutes later. She was looking at his shirts on their hangers.

"These are real expensive, right? They're paying you OK, aren't they?"

"Sure."

"How long do you reckon you're going to keep the job?"

"Another week or so. There's another one to get rid of. Different bank, same job. Same type of asshole. Him and Reichman are the two worst on Wall Street."

"And then? Back to Ohio with me?" She said it almost hopefully.

"There's one more to take care of after that," he told her. "These ratings agencies. Someone in there is sticking prime labels on cheap steaks and helping them rip off people like you and my sister. Probably not somebody. Probably a team."

"So what are you going to do?"

"Send them a message. Haven't decided what yet, but these bastards need waking up."

"Then Ohio?"

"Then back to Ohio. With you and the kids, if you want me after all this."

"I think I do."

Hampton nursed her drink for a little longer, hoping that Tommy would come back, or that one of the other traders would come over and give her some more information, but it didn't look as though it was going to happen.

She didn't feel like smoking one of her cigars tonight. In any case, she'd be given a hard time of it when she got home.

It was raining hard when she looked outside, so she indulged in a little luxury and caught a cab to the brownstone where she rented a tiny apartment.

"Honey, I'm home!" she called as she walked through the door.

Liz, her partner of five years, met her. "You didn't say when you'd be back, so I haven't cooked anything. There's some of last night's lasagna you can nuke if you want."

"Have you eaten?"

"Some cheese and crackers. Had a client lunch

which filled me up." Liz worked as an account executive in a PR agency. "You?"

"Corned beef on rye at my desk. The usual. It's not fair. Why aren't you enormous, with all the lunches you eat all the time?" Liz, while not supermodel skinny, was certainly far from overweight, while Kendra was continually fighting a tendency to plumpness.

"Because I get down to the gym regularly, sweetheart, while you're sitting at the keyboard all the time." They'd had this conversation many times, with Liz, a determined keep-fit addict, always trying to get her partner to share her obsession.

"Honey, if I lifted weights and ran marathons all day, I'd just end up like Arnie Schwarzenegger, all muscles and bulges, not slim at all. It's just me."

"Love you all the same," Liz said, and hugged her friend, planting a kiss on the top of her head.

Kendra laughed. "Lasagna it is. Did you get a movie to watch tonight?"

Liz held up a DVD. "'The Blind Side' — it's about a high school football player."

"Now why would I be interested in that, sweetie? Since when was I a football fan?"

"It's based on a book by Michael Lewis."

"Oh." Michael Lewis' book, *Liar's Poker*, describing the excesses of 1980s Wall Street, had been one of the factors propelling Kendra into the financial services sector. "We'll give it a shot."

Actually, Kendra thought, as slipped under the

duvet a few hours later, the lasagna had been better than the movie. Not one of Lewis' best efforts, though she guessed the book might be better than the movie.

Liz was already in bed, tapping away at a spreadsheet. She closed the laptop and reached out to Kendra. "What sort of day did you have?"

"Weird. Rather horrible, in fact. One of my pets was found dead in his car."

Liz knew that Kendra's "pets" were the sources for her articles. "Sounds grim. Did you like him?"

"I suppose I did. He was a pretty foul-mouthed specimen, but he was funny most of the time, and he certainly gave good phone."

"What did he die of? Heart attack or something?"

"No, that's what upset me more than anything else. He was found shot in his car. Two shots to the head, and it wasn't a robbery, either. I talked to some of his people earlier, and they swear up and down that the Mob wasn't involved in this one. No reason for him to be involved with them, they say."

"Is there a story there?"

"There would be if his bank wasn't so paranoid about the story getting out. If I tell the story, they're going to want to know where it came from."

"Which bank?"

Kendra told her. "They're one of your clients, aren't they?"

"Yeah. They're paranoid, all right. Reckon

you'd get more out of the police?"

"I would if I knew anyone there."

"Let me ask. We ran a campaign for them a couple of months back. I'm guessing I can get someone there to contact you. You really want to know more about this?"

Kendra thought a minute. "Yes, I think I do." She told Liz what she'd been told about the Swiss banker who'd also been found dead. Liz shuddered. "So there's some maniac running round killing off bankers?"

"Sounds like it."

"Glad you're not working in a bank any more, sweetie?"

"I suppose I am, come to think of it."

ABOUT 10:30 THE NEXT MORNING, Hampton was eating her regular morning bagel at her desk (she started work early, and usually forgot to eat breakfast, or was too busy to grab anything until halfway through the morning) when her Blackberry beeped.

"I found you a wonderful man – Phil – call him after 5 tonight. Liz xxx," the message read, followed by a phone number.

She smiled to herself. Liz had a sense of humor that was all her own. What did she want with a wonderful man, when she had Liz? Still, if Liz said he was wonderful, the odds were that he wasn't completely toxic.

Come five o'clock, she was ready to leave. It had been a slow news day, and for once there were no stories on her desk waiting to be filed. She'd made discreet enquiries around the office, but no-one else seemed to have heard anything about the dead traders.

She called the number that Liz had sent her, and found herself speaking to a voice that she could only describe as "chocolatey".

"I'm a friend of Liz Shapiro's," she told him. "I work for FNS, and I'd like some off-the-record information."

"Sure, sweetheart."

Sweetheart? Was she going to have to beat him off with a stick? "So what can you tell me?"

"Nothing over the phone. I'll meet you at the Italian place — Harry's on Gold — at seven. You eat pizza, I hope?"

"I know where you mean, and yeah, I eat pizza. Try and stop me. I'll book a table in my name — Kendra Hampton. See you there."

"Sure."

SEVEN O'CLOCK CAME, and Kendra was sitting nursing a Manhattan, when a tall gangly man came by her table.

"Hi, I'm Phil Kerrigan," he introduced himself. She looked him up and down. Quite smartly dressed in a blue sports coat and striped shirt, and what she thought of as "proper" shoes.

"Hi there." She invited him to sit opposite her at the table, and he took a seat.

"What are you drinking?" he asked, pointing to her nearly empty glass. He ordered two Manhattans.

"Thanks for agreeing to see me," she said.

"My pleasure. Liz and her team did a good job for the Department, and I don't mind repaying favors. Liz is a sweet lady."

"She is," she replied, trying to inject some meaning into her speech. He noticed.

"OK, I think I get you, but I won't pry. I'm only a guy in Records. I don't wear a badge or a gun or anything, but I do hear things."The drinks arrived. "So, Liz said you were interested in that Wall Street honcho we found in his Ferrari. Cheers."

"Cheers. Yes, I heard something about it from one of the guys at his firm, but you know these people. They're scared to talk in case their bosses hear that they've been telling tales out of school."

"So how much did he tell you exactly? And why do you want to know more?"

"Answering the last one first, because I think there may be a story in it somewhere. Liz told you what I do for a living?"

"She did. But this is strictly off the record, right? You can live with that?"

She nodded, and told Phil what she had been told by Tommy the trader at the next desk to Charlie's.

"Yep, that's true as far as it goes. By the way, shall we order? I skipped lunch."

Kendra had learned by experience that the subject being interviewed over a meal should choose the food – they felt more in control and less pressured, and were more willing to talk than if she dictated the menu. As it happened, he chose the same sort of meal – pizza and salad – that she would have done, and she was happy to go along with that and a bottle of red to wash it down.

"But there's more?"

"Yes, and this is the bit that we didn't tell the bank. Charles Sanfion had called us earlier in the week to report that he was being watched."

"And you guys didn't take him seriously? One of those rich Wall Street Masters of the Universe types, and you did nothing?"

He held up a warning hand. "Time out. He didn't try to pull rank on us or anything. Just gave us his name and an address. Sure, it was a swank area, but not that swank. Two, the guy was wasted when he called us. Sounded as though he'd had several too many on the way home. We get a few of those calls every day. The reports usually get thrown in the circular filing cabinet at worst, or shoved to the bottom of the pile at best."

"But there is a record of this call?"

"Sure there is."

"And who did he say was following him, then?"

"Would you believe that he thought it was a black dude? Like, around eighty percent of the calls like that we get from white guys, it's a black dude following them. The other twenty percent are Hispanics. Funny how white guys never follow white guys, isn't it?"

"So he was being followed by a black guy? And did you hear from him again?"

Phil shook his head. "There's nothing on file. We can assume he didn't."

"Well, if eighty percent of these callers report that they're being followed by black guys, what's special about this one?"

"He was able to give some sort of description. Quite a good one, actually. Tall guy, mid-thirties, well built, very short hair, very smart casual clothing, dark windbreaker, light slacks."

"Only describes a few thousand people." The food arrived, and they started to eat. "So what's special about this one?"

"First off, he didn't sound like your usual street punk or gang member. One phrase that Sanfion used to describe him was 'military'. It's in the transcript."

"So we're down to a few hundred suspects, maybe. Lot of vets out there."

"Okay, here's the other interesting bit. Did you hear that the Swiss bank opposite Sanfion's place lost a guy in the same way? Two shots to the head while he was sitting in his car?"

She nodded. "I was told something about it."

"Not a coincidence. This guy had also reported he was being stalked. Gave a description."

"Same guy, right?"

"Yep. Matched the other perfectly."

They made their way through the pizza in silence, Hampton considering what she'd just been told.

"OK, I was told these weren't robberies. Correct?" she said.

"Correct. These guys were found with folding money stuffed into their mouths."

"I was told that. Ten-dollar bills, right?"

"Yep. Three ten-dollar bills in each case. We're dealing with a sick fuck here. Sorry about the language."

"I've heard worse." She smiled, and appeared to be lost in thought for a while, and then sat up with a start. "Thirty pieces of silver," she said.

"Uh?"

"The reward Judas got for betraying Jesus. Don't you know your Bible? Thirty pieces of silver, the traitor's reward."

"So we're looking for a religious nut who's a veteran, and fits the physical description the two vics provided?"

"Needn't be a religious nut. Just someone who knows his literary and religious references."

"Okay. I hear you." He paused, and appeared to be waiting for something.

"What do you want from me?"

He smiled. "You're a reporter, right?"

"Journalist." She preferred the term.

"Whatever. This is a Homicide case. None of us knows shit about Wall Street. What do these dudes actually do for a living?"

"Well, I don't know who the Swiss guy was, so I can't tell you that, but Sanfion trades — traded, rather, derivatives."

"What's that in English?"

"When there's something whose price depends on the price of something else, that's a derivative. So for example, suppose I want to buy futures in the Nikkei—"

"You're losing me already."

"Okay. Buying a future basically means you're placing a bet on whether the price of something will go up or down. The Nikkei is the Japanese stock index. Like the Dow. So if you think the Nikkei will go up, you'd like to bet on this, and be allowed to buy at today's prices, which are cheaper than the prices you think they will be in the future. That's going long. Going short is the reverse – you're betting prices are going to fall. So you borrow something where you think the price is going to drop, you sell at today's prices, and when the price has gone down, you buy back whatever it is you borrowed at the new lower price and give it back."

Phil scratched his head. "It's weird."

"Those are the easy ones. It gets a lot weirder and more complicated."

"Don't bother explaining. So what sort of things was Sanfion trading?"

"He was doing mortgages. Or rather all kinds of derivatives based around home mortgages. A pretty risky business."

"Safe as houses, I'd have thought." He chuckled at his own wit.

"It would be if the mortgages were real."

"Say that again. These guys are selling fake mortgages?"

"Yep. Folks who have no right being offered any kind of mortgage are being offered crazy money, at terms they can't afford. There's a lot of foreclosures out there right now."

"Well, no-one is forcing these people to take out the mortgages, right?"

"Of course not. But someone comes along, waves a photo of a fancy great house in front of you and tells you that this can be yours if you only sign on the dotted line here, and not to worry about all these fancy figures and things – they'll get filled in for you back at the office—"

"You're telling me that's what's happening?"

"Yeah, and no-one wants to admit it. It gets worse, though."

"How does it get worse than that?"

"These are pretty crappy loans to be making, aren't they? They know a lot of them are never going to be repaid. So they sell them."

"You can sell loans?"

"Sure. Happens all the time. It's the basis of modern capitalism, playing with other people's money that you don't have anyway."

"My head's spinning. Aren't you in love with all of this stuff, though? I mean, Liz said to me that this is how you make your living."

"If I'm to be honest with you, I don't know how much longer I can keep doing this. The more I learn about these things, the less happy I am about them. There is some really evil stuff going on here in the mortgage market and I think it's still happening or even getting worse."

"Sounds like it. Tell me, if these mortgages are so crappy – I mean, if no-one is ever going to re-pay them – how can you persuade people to buy them? And who are the suckers who are buying them, anyway?"

"Pension funds, foreign banks, whoever. And they really don't know what they're buying. Listen, you go to the supermarket, you buy a steak, right? It's labeled as 'prime' or 'choice' or 'select', isn't it? Well, the same sort of thing hap-pens to anything that the big boys on Wall Street are selling. They go along to one of the rating agencies, and they get a label stuck on the mortgage bonds or whatever it is they're peddling, and they can go out and sell it."

"So?"

"Someone has been sticking 'prime' labels on these piles of crap. And of course, they make a lot of money when they sell these things. So the pressure was on to stick the expensive labels on the crap."

"And when the shit hits the fan?"

"There's one part of one insurance company, AIG, which actually insures the banks against these things going bad."

"And if they do go bad?"

"We're going to be in the middle of the mother of all shitstorms. Some of these Wall Street firms are in this shit right the way up to their eyebrows."

"I'm beginning to understand what's been going on. Thanks for letting me in on the secrets. It's not exactly cheerful news."

She shrugged. "It's no big secret, really. Just a matter of connecting the dots. Anyway, returning to Charles Sanfion, that's what he did for a living. Traded crappy mortgage bonds."

"Could you find out what the other guy – the Swiss guy – did at his place?"

"I could, if I knew his name."

Phil smiled and passed over a card. "My name and e-mail and office phone and cellphone are on this side. I wrote the dear departed's name on the back."

She took the card. "You told me you were in Records? You get a card to give out?"

He grinned. "I lied. I'm actually a Homicide detective, and I'm on this case – these cases."

She felt angry at being deceived. "Why? Why the hell did you lie?"

"People open up more if they don't know what I am and what I do."

"I can understand that, I guess. I suppose I play the same sort of game sometimes when I'm writing a story and talking to sources. Doesn't mean I like myself for doing it, or you for doing it to me."

Still angry, she turned the card over and read the name written on the other side. "Carl Reichman. No, that rings no bells with me, I'm afraid. I could find out, I guess. I have some contacts at that place. You think there may be a connection?"

"I'm sure there is a connection. We know there is, from the description of the stalker and the way these people died. The question is whether there's another connection based around Wall Street, and if there is, how many other people are going to get their two bullets and thirty pieces of silver."

"Would you be prepared to help us, like you did just now? A bit of background to help us understand what's going on?"

"What's in it for me? I suppose that's a pretty typical New York answer, but I have to ask, don't

I?"

"Might be able to arrange to get you off parking tickets."

"Don't drive a car."

He ignored her words. "More to the point, you'll be the first to know the inside story on the Wall Street murders when we find out more about what's been going on. You'll have at least twenty-four hours over anyone else."

"Sounds reasonable. I'll let you know."

"You called me from your office. Got a cell number where I can reach you?"

"You'll know it when I call you from there."

"I get it." He sounded resigned.

"I will call you, don't worry. I'll find out more about the Swiss guy and let you know what he was up to. Out of interest, have there been any more killings like this, or have there only been these two?"

"I heard something about a few in Ohio a month or so back. No money in the mouth, but the same two .45 bullets to the head. There was one rather bizarre thing about a couple of the killings."

"A couple? How many were there?"

"About half a dozen, all the same cause of death. Some in Akron or thereabouts, and some in Columbus."

"And all connected?"

"Two of them worked for the same company — a local bank."

Kendra raised her eyebrows. "Interesting. And

the others?"

"I don't have the details. I can find out and swap you for what you find out about this Reichman guy if you're interested."

"Maybe. What was the bizarre thing you were going to tell me?"

"I wasn't going to tell you. Not while we're sitting in a restaurant. Some time later, maybe. Can I walk you home?"

"You can, but I warn you that you won't be invited in for a coffee or anything like that. My partner, Liz, is waiting for me, and she gets a little antsy if I bring home visitors late at night, especially men."

He nodded. "Understood. The offer to walk you home still stands, though." A gentleman.

HAMPTON SAT AT HER DESK the next morning and thought about what she'd been told the previous night. When she'd arrived at home, having been escorted by Phil as promised, Liz had been intrigued by her account of her "date".

"It sounds as though you should invite him here some time, if you think he can be trusted to behave himself," she had said. "He sounds all right."

"You didn't work with him when you were doing that project for them, then?"

"He was one of the ones we did an interview with and put on video. He came over pretty well, and I thought he might be the best person for you to talk to."

THIS MORNING, Hampton decided she was going to look a little deeper into what Phil Kerrigan had told her. There might just be some sort of link between the Ohio murders and the Wall Street ones, and it would do her career no harm at all if she was the one to make it all public.

She picked up the phone and dialed the cellphone of one of her former Bear colleagues, who now worked at the Swiss bank.

"Hi there, it's Kendra. Yeah, fine. Yeah, still with FNS. Yeah, tough sometimes, but I don't miss the assholes on the trading floor. You? Too bad. Hey, got a question about one of your guys. Carl Reichman. No, I'd heard that. Where did he work, then? What desk? OK, thanks. Yes, let's do dinner soon. Stay in touch. Ciao." She put the phone down and sighed. It seemed that Carl Reichman had worked on the mortgage bond trading desk. The dots were joining up.

She hadn't exactly promised Phil Kerrigan that she would contact him, but she'd come close to doing so. Time she told him what she had found out. She picked up her cellphone.

"Well, well," he said, after she had told him. "Someone doesn't like these people, it would seem."

"Can you find out more about the Ohio murders and let me know?"

"I guess I can. You talked a bit about ratings agencies yesterday. Tell me more."

"Okay, when you buy something, you always like to check it out, don't you? If it's a car or something like that that you're buying, you can go out for a spin in it, kick the tires, whatever?"

"Yeah."

"You can't do that with something like a bond or a derivative. All you've got is the word of the guy who's selling it to you, and he's not exactly going to be neutral about things, is he?"

"Okay?"

"So that's where the rating agencies come into it. There's two or three of them, and they look at the things – the products – that the banks and the investment houses are selling off, and they put a sticker on them."

"What sort of sticker?"

"Well, let's say that they're US Treasury bonds –T-bills. The USA isn't going to collapse any time soon, so there's no real risk involved when you buy these. They're going to make money whatever happens, and they'll get a top rating, let's call it Aaa+, like one of the ratings agencies does. But suppose that there's a uranium mining operation in the Sudan. Pretty risky place. Always wars going on around there, and uranium's a great target. That is, assuming that there's any there in the first place. So if you put your money in there, there's a pretty fair chance you'll lose it. That'll probably get a rating of Ccc minus, the lowest."

"So these guys doing the ratings must be pretty shit-hot at what they do?"

"I'd like to think so."

"But?"

"But there's a lot of stuff coming out of there which is getting ratings much higher than I think it should."

"Know anyone there to talk to?"

"Why?"

"Seems to me there's a chance that the guy who killed our two traders is someone who lost money on these mortgage bonds. Maybe if we went through the list of customers of bonds which were overrated, we could find a match somewhere in the lists."

"They'd never admit they overrated a bond, and the banks aren't going to give up their customer lists just like that," she told him. "Nice try, though."

"Okay. I'll be in touch about Ohio."

When he'd rung off, Hampton thought a bit more about what she'd just said. It was true that none of the rating agencies would go on the record, but she might be able to call in a favor from one of her friends who worked there.

"Pat?" she asked. "How's things? Yeah, same old, same old. What about you? Really? Then you're just the person I want to talk to. No, no, it will be off the record. Come round and have dinner with Liz and me at our place. Tomorrow sound good to you? Eight? Sure. You're still vegetarian, right? No problem at all. Great. See ya."

She called Liz and told her to expect a dinner guest the next night. "Your cashew mushroom loaf would be a great idea for Patricia."

"Just Patricia?"

"Shall I invite Phil Kerrigan?" She'd meant it as a joke, but Liz seemed to take it seriously.

"Yeah, why not?"

Actually, why not indeed? She had a hunch

that Patricia and Phil would get on together, and though she usually didn't like playing matchmaker, it might help ease conversation a little if there was another at the table.

She called Phil to invite him, and he accepted gratefully. "Much appreciated, I assure you, and I will have some interesting news for you about Ohio. Unless you'd prefer to hear it now?"

"It can wait."

TWENTY-ONE: SEPTEMBER 2007

PHIL ARRIVED. Kendra watched his embarrassment with some amusement as he finally worked out her relationship with Liz, but he seemed to cheer up when Patricia arrived.

Patricia wasn't Kendra's type, but she certainly did seem to attract men, with long dark hair, all the right curves in the places that men found attractive, and a face that appeared to be screaming for a man to protect her. Not that Patricia needed protection, Kendra knew. She was as tough as any man on Wall Street, and could outswear and outcuss any of them at the drop of a hat.

Tonight she was wearing a dress that exposed a good deal of her top, and left little of her legs to the imagination. Had Liz told her that Phil was coming round? Kendra wondered.

Phil and Patricia settled down on the sofa together, with glasses of the chilled Chardonnay that Phil had brought with him. Kendra perched on a straight-backed chair facing them. Liz had taken herself off to the kitchen with her glass of wine.

"You told us that you had some news about Ohio?" Kendra said.

"Speak up," Liz called from the kitchen. "I want to know what this is all about."

"What's this about Ohio?" Patricia asked.

Phil started to speak, but Kendra interrupted him. "You know Charles Sanfion?" she asked.

"You mean that mortgage bond trader who killed himself the other day?"

Phil raised his eyebrows. "Is that what you heard?"

"That's what they're saying. They're all talking about it."

"That one," said Kendra. "And Carl Reichman?"

"Oh him. Asshole Reichman from that Swiss bank? Met him once, and he made a pass. Not so much a pass as a drunken fumble. What about him?"

"You know he died, a week before Sanfion?"

"No. How?"

"Same way as Sanfion," said Phil. "Two bullets to the head, and thirty dollars in tens stuffed into his mouth."

"So you're saying Sanfion was killed? And this other asshole, Reichman, too?"

Phil nodded. "We're assuming that. It's a strange kind of suicide who shoots himself in the head and there's no gun to be found."

"And thirty bucks stuffed into their mouths. Thirty pieces of silver?"

"That's what I thought, too," Kendra told her. "Whoever did this had something against mortgage traders. Lost their money investing in the bonds, perhaps."

"What's with Ohio?" Liz called from the kitchen.

"I'm getting there," Phil said. "I'm not sure that we have to look at the Street."

"I think we do," Kendra told him. "You've got two deaths here on Wall Street. There's a link between them, and the link is mortgage bonds."

"So is the link to Ohio," said Phil. "There's been a few of these 'double-tap' murders around the Akron and Columbus area. And some of them are pretty gruesome. You ladies up to hearing the details?" He stopped, and noticed the sudden chill in the atmosphere. "Hey, I'm trying to be nice here. Would you *people* like to hear the details?"

"Okay, go ahead."

"There's six of them that we know about. Same MO. Double shot to the head, and some sort of ritual humiliation, I guess you'd have to call it, in each case. Sure you want to hear?"

"Sure," Liz called from the kitchen. Kendra and Patricia exchanged glances and nodded.

"Okay, here we go. The first one's maybe the most difficult one. Two men, found dead together. One a pastor, one some sort of mortgage sales guy."

"You mean he was selling mortgages to the homeowners?" Kendra asked.

"Yes, and typically they weren't the sort of

people who should be taking out mortgages."

"Subprime junk," said Patricia.

"If that's what you want to call it, yes."

"Seems the pastor was telling his flock to buy these mortgages. Local cops looked at his bank records, and it seems he was getting some kick-backs from the shyster. That's not the worst. These guys were really into sick porn. Pedo stuff, involving rape and torture of little kids. They were part of some sort of online network that traded these things. They made DVDs of these things. And they weren't just watching this stuff, they were making it."

"Ugh," said Patricia. "You're making my skin crawl."

"If any guys deserved to die, it was them. I don't usually say things like that, but in this case..." He shook his head. "And they found one with the other's dick— sorry, penis—"

"It's all right, we've all heard those things called dicks before," said Patricia.

"Okay, then. Both found naked from the waist down. One with the other guy's dick in his mouth. The other guy's balls were pretty much crushed, by the way." He shook his head. "Makes me cross my legs just thinking about it."

"Who was doing what to who, then?"

"The pastor was the active one, shall we say. Except neither was terribly active, really. Each of them with a couple of bullets in the head. The cops who saw the scene reckoned the pastor was forced into doing it and then shot. That's two deaths."

"More wine?" Kendra asked them.

"Yes," from Liz in the kitchen. "I need it."

"Me too," said Patricia.

"Well," Phil went on when Kendra had returned and refilled all their glasses. "The next two were some skanky meth addict and his girl. Same thing. Double shot to the head. Same gun that killed the pastor and his friend, ballistics reckon. He'd messed his pants before he was shot – don't ask me how they work these things out, but they say they can – and he'd been standing there for some time by the look of the grass and the footprints. There'd been a car parked nearby, and they reckon he was shot from there. She was just shot where she was standing, or probably running away."

"You're not telling me that the meth head was selling mortgages?"

"No, but he'd been picked up the day before for the murder of a woman and four kids who'd been kicked out of their house for not paying their mortgage. The local cops let him go. His prints were all over a knife that was found there, but there was no proof he'd actually done it. They didn't think they could make it stick in court, with his girl swearing up and down that he was innocent."

"Apart from the fact that this woman and her kids had been thrown out of the house, is there any other connection?"

"Yeah. Police were pretty sure he was part of

this kiddy porn business. Supplying the raw material, as it were." He let his words sink in.

"Sickening stuff," said Kendra.

"It's horrible," agreed Patricia. "I can see why you didn't want to tell us straight away." Her hand moved to cover Phil's. Kendra noticed that he didn't seem to mind that at all.

"Well, given what they knew and what they found out about these scumbags, the police seemed to be glad rather than otherwise that they were no longer around. They weren't going to push the case too hard. If the guy who did it walked in and gave himself up, they would have to do something, but otherwise, they wouldn't bother, except for the other two killings."

"And they were?"

"Two employees of a local bank that sold the mortgages. One was the loan officer of a branch. She was shot in the parking lot of the bank, conveniently just out of sight of a CCTV camera. Apparently she was some sort of martial arts black belt, but it didn't seem to have done her much good."

"Same gun?"

Phil nodded. "Yep. Ballistics say that the gun used was the same one as on the other four, and on the sixth one. He worked at the bank headquarters in Columbus, and sold on the mortgages to Wall Street."

"Something nasty in the way he died?"

"Same way of killing. He was shot in his car. He was taking his kids to school, and from what we can tell, he was carjacked. The killer told the kids to get out of the car, so they didn't see his father shot. There's some sort of description of the killer. Tall, black, wearing a windbreaker."

"Could be any one of hundreds, thousands, couldn't it?"

"Right. Not exactly helpful. But it matches the description that Reichman and Sanfion gave us. And, get this, the ballistics on these Wall Street killings match the ones from the Ohio killings."

"Dinner's ready," Liz called.

"Sorry if I've spoiled your appetites," Phil said, as they seated themselves around the table.

"You'll have to do better than that to put us off Liz's cooking," Kendra told him. "Though it is pretty horrible, isn't it?"

"So we have this tall black guy wearing a windbreaker going round after anyone to do with mortgages?" said Patricia. "I'm scared. I mean, I deal with mortgages. I'm the one who does the preliminary analysis at the rating agency that gives them their final ratings."

"And?"

"They're fixed," Patricia told them all. "Look, I don't want this to get out, as it's more than my job's worth. It's a pretty shitty job, perhaps, and it doesn't pay that great, but it's a job, okay? The banks come in with these piles of mortgages that they put together into these bonds, and it's my job to pass judgement on them. Well, a lot of them are just piles of steaming crap, to be honest, pardon my French and all that shit, but they're crap. I can't imagine anyone wanting to look at them. Think of a kosher butcher in Saudi Arabia. Think of his business prospects. Well, I tell you they're fucking golden compared to what I see. Sometimes I just know that they're shitty. I ask for the tapes—"

"The what?"

"The evidence of the mortgages. The details. Are we talking decent housing or crappy McMansions? What are the people like? How the hell am I supposed to put any kind of value on these things without knowing the details? And when I ask, I'm told I can't have them. And stuff I know is crap gets rated with the top ratings. I put in a report that these are shit, and I see them going out of the door with Aaa ratings on them."

"It's as bad as that?" Kendra asked.

"It's worse, really. And there's billions and billions of dollars going on this stuff. Some of it's not even real, I swear. These mortgages aren't real mortgages, I'm sure. Someone's going to get burned really badly, I tell you. One of the big firms is going to be biting the dust some time in the next twelve months. Maybe more than one. Hard to tell. But if you've got any money in stocks or anything like that, I'd take it out now, and put the cash under the mattress. It's pretty wild out there."

They ate in silence for a while. "Awesome nut loaf, Liz," Phil said. "I'm not usually into vegetarian food, but this is pretty amazing."

"Thanks, Phil. I've been thinking about what

you've told us. There's a pretty smart guy out there, who knows how to join up the dots, it seems. He's found out about the banks, the Wall Street connections, and those kiddie porn scumbags who were selling the mortgages. Is the next stop going to be Patricia's ratings agency?"

Patricia shivered. "Liz, what the hell are you saying?"

"She's got a point," Phil told her. "There's someone out there who's carrying a grudge, and it wouldn't surprise me if he's working his way up the chain."

"Up?" Patricia laughed bitterly. "I won't tell you want I get paid, but I can tell you it's a fucking sight less than the assholes on the trading floor, or even their grunts in the back office. You'd think that actually rating these things would be a more responsible job than selling them, wouldn't you, and that you'd get paid properly for doing it. I can tell you it doesn't work out that way."

"Up or down or sideways, though, Patricia, I'd let your bosses know that they might be next."

"Or I might be next?" She shivered again.

"I'll take care of you," Phil said.

I bet you will, Kendra thought to herself, amused, despite the situation. Liz really did have a point. "Phil, what you're saying is that we have a lone nut going round looking for anyone on Wall Street connected with the mortgage bond business, and they're all in danger?"

"Maybe not just anyone, but yeah, I would say that anyone in the business is at risk."

"More than just the usual crossing the road type of risk?"

"Yeah."

"Then do you think it would help if I wrote a story about this, and put it out? Maybe let the guy know you've got a lead on him, and make him back off a bit?"

"That's a thought. Don't quote me or mention my name, though," Phil said.

"Or me, for God's sake," said Patricia.

"I'm used to doing that. You'll both just be 'unnamed sources' or something."

"That's fine. Yes, you might keep Patricia safe with that idea. If the guy reads that we know so much about him, then he might well just go home to Ohio and we'll all be safe."

"I'll ask my editor tomorrow to let me work on it. Patricia, is it really OK if I put in something about what you told us about the bond ratings? Not mentioning you or the agency by name, of course."

"I guess so. Maybe it will help shake things up a bit. I'd like to think so, anyway."

" I might even go to Ohio and see what I can find there." Kendra's face took on what Liz called her 'planning look', which she wore whenever she was mapping out her writing.

"Snap out of it, Ken," said Liz. "We have guests."

"Okay," said Kendra, and the evening proceeded, with some flirtation between Phil and Patricia, who left very much as a couple.

"Thanks for making it such a success, Liz,"

Kendra said, throwing her arms around her partner's neck and kissing her.

"I think we've made two people rather happy," Liz smiled back. "At least for one night – maybe longer."

TWENTY-TWO: OCTOBER 2007

KENDRA'S EDITOR agreed that the story would make an interesting break from the usual bond analysis, and gave her permission to go to Ohio.

She returned a few days later, full of news.

"He's a smart one, Liz," she said. "I went to the places where those two murdered bank employees worked. The receptionists remembered this tall black guy – military-looking, some of them said – coming in to see them both, a couple of days apart. One in Akron and one in Columbus. They couldn't give any description beyond the obvious, but he was definitely checking them out for future reference. For what it's worth, they were both complete assholes at work. Tallman in the head office at Columbus. It doesn't seem he's missed much by anyone there. The woman loan officer in Akron, Leonora Allenby, sounds like a right bitch. Once I'd got past the formalities of 'how much we'll miss her', it was obvious that she was one cold-hearted scumbag. Maybe not in the same class as the pastor and his friend, but no angel, for sure."

"And the pastor and the meth heads?"

"Cops aren't even bothering to investigate the meth heads. Good riddance to bad rubbish seems to be the order of the day there. As for the pastor, they're closing the books on that one, too. The Feds are looking at the child porno ring. I heard things about those people that made my skin crawl. I won't tell you, sweetie, but if I wake up screaming in the night, it's because of what the cops in charge of the case told me. I thought it was just a few sickos, but it's a lot of people, and I was told there are some big names involved, but of course, they won't tell me any more details."

"So the guy's a hero for getting rid of public nuisances and assholes?"

"That's how the police in Ohio are treating it, it seems. But he's a murderer, Liz, let's not forget, and some of our friends may be in danger."

"Are you going to tell Phil what you discovered?"

"I guess he knows most of it already. Maybe not about the bankers being total assholes, but everything else. I'm going to Sanfion's bank and the Swiss bank tomorrow morning. Write the story in the afternoon, and with luck it will hit the site the morning after."

"You're not worried he'll come after you?" Liz sounded concerned.

"Sweetie, I'm just setting out the facts. I don't have a name for him. It may be that he feels his work is done, and he's not going to kill any more. I'll be fine."

The next day took her to the bank where Charles Sanfion worked. As she had half-expected, there was nothing to be gained from the corporate communications staff. Still, Tommy had told her when all this started that she was free to quote him anonymously. She could still remember what he had said and decided to use that in her piece.

The Swiss bank was just as uncommunicative (Swiss bankers? What did you expect? she told herself). In this case, she didn't even get past the senior security guy.

He was more than a little intimidating – a tall, well-built black man in a beautifully-cut suit and a military air about him. He introduced himself only as "Henry", without a last name. She noticed a Marine Corps ring on one hand, but refrained from asking any questions about it.

"Did you know Mr. Reichman?" she asked him.

"Yes, ma'am, I did." Very cool and correct, not giving away more than he had to.

There was something vaguely familiar about his face. "Have we met?"

"I'm sure I would remember you, ma'am." A smile which flickered briefly and then vanished as if it had never been.

"Strange," she mused. "Pardon my curiosity, but may I ask how you met Mr. Reichman?"

"We met at a social event." This guy wasn't going to give anything away. Something told her that fluttering her eyelashes at him and using her feminine charms was going to have as much effect on him as it would do on the coffee machine in the corner.

The rest of the "interview", if you could call it that, consisted of similar stonewalling tactics. All requests for further information were politely, but firmly, refused, and she knew from experience that there was no point in pushing matters further.

"Thank you," she said, long before the thirty minutes she had been allotted was up. "You've been most helpful."

Again that instant smile as he stood up. He moved to hold the door open for her. "I know I haven't been at all helpful. But I'm afraid that's my job, ma'am."

Despite herself, she smiled back. "I understand. Thank you … Henry."

Once back at her desk, she called Phil. "You'd have more luck with the Mafia," she told him. "These guys are giving nothing away." She passed on the information about the two Ohio bankers.

"So he only kills assholes?" Phil said.

"So far. I wouldn't call Charles Sanfion a complete asshole, though. He had his good points, and could be charming. Most of the time he was a bastard, though, agreed. Still haven't been able to get anything definite on Reichman, though. Shall I send you a copy of what I've written before I send it on to the editor?"

She could almost hear Phil shrug. "Sure, if you

want to."

"I'd like to. I want to make sure I've got the story right."

"When do you think you can let me have it?"

"Couple of hours. I'll send it to the Yahoo! mail account you have."

The story wrote itself. It was a pretty easy lead, and the headline, "Death Stalks Wall Street", seemed suitably dramatic to her. She included the Ohio material, and gave what details she know of the Wall Street deaths. Phil corrected one or two small matters related to police terminology and ranks, and she sent the corrected copy to her editor, who okayed it, and sent it to the layout people who would turn it into a Web page.

"Good work," his email back to her said.

THE KILLING of Charles Sanfion hadn't made the press, rather to Powers' disappointment. He'd rather hoped that someone would put two and two together and make four, but no-one seemed capable of doing that. It seemed that he would have to somehow send the message himself when he took care of the rating agency.

Jeanine was enjoying New York, and Powers was enjoying her company. The sex was great, but she also brought an order and a peace to his life that he hadn't experienced for a long time, if ever. Every night she called her sister in Ohio, and talked to her children, without mentioning where she was, or who she was staying with.

After Sanfion's death, she was getting ready to go back, with or without him. "I can't leave them with Brandi all this time. I know you've got unfinished business here."

"It's going to get finished real soon," he told her. "I think I'd better do it soon. I had some sort of reporter coming and asking questions earlier today. If the story of the Wall Street murders, or whatever they want to call it, gets out and people start to look out for little things, there's probably some way they can trace things back to me. I hope not, but you never know."

"Reporter from where? *New York Times?*"

"No, one of those specialist places that concentrates on financial news. FNS. Everyone has one of their screens on their desks at the bank. It will be on their website tomorrow, if it's coming out at all."

The next morning before breakfast saw him tapping away at the laptop computer the bank issued to him. Jeanine was still asleep.

"Holy shit!" he exclaimed, when he read the article on the FNS site, loud enough to wake Jeanine.

"What is it?" she said, getting out of bed and standing behind him.

"They've worked out that there's a connection between the killings in Ohio and the killings on Wall Street. Ballistics, damn it. I should have changed guns."

"So? None of that points in your direction, does it?"

"Look." He pointed to part of the screen. "'Before their deaths, both Reichman and Sanfion are believed to have reported being stalked by a large well-built man with short hair, wearing a dark hooded windbreaker, believed to be African-American.' That's me, right?"

"Sure it is, honey, but it's also fifty thousand other folks in this city. Relax. You are Mister Henry Powers," (they'd eventually learned each other's last names) "the deputy chief of security at the bank. You're the dude who wears these sharp suits and snazzy ties, right? You're not some hobo in a dirty windbreaker who goes round stalking traders, are you?"

"Yeah, but… Maybe it's just me being paranoid, but it seems the less that they have to go on, the better it is for me – for us," he corrected himself. "Remember, you found me, easily enough."

"Sure, but I wasn't looking for a killer. But yeah, I see your point. Something tells me, though, that they're not going to worry too hard about that scumbag pastor and his friend, or the two meth heads. I guess the police would give you a medal for that. Look at this bit here. It seems like they've cracked a nationwide pedophile ring thanks to you offing those two dickweeds."

He continued reading. "Now how in hell did she guess that the rating agencies were next? Look at this."

She read out, "'There are rumors floating around the Street that the workers at the rating agencies, who are said by some to have given overly optimistic ratings to some mortgage-backed securities, may be the killer's next target.' Then there's a whole lot of stuff I don't understand about these bond things, but it seems she's saying what you told me – they're a complete load of crap and the people selling them are assholes. Have you heard any of these rumors about the agencies being a target?"

He shook his head. "No. And I guess I'd hear them first."

"Then she's just guessed lucky, then. Who is she?"

"Youngish, tough-looking, but quite cute with it, worked with the banks before becoming a journalist. Knows her shit, I'd say. Oh, and she's a dyke. Lives with her girlfriend of four or five years."

"How the hell do you know all this?"

"There's some great research tools there at the bank, and journalists are pretty public figures."

"So what's all this mean, then?"

"It means I should do whatever I'm going to do, and then get the hell out of Dodge."

"And what are you going to do?"

"I'm going to set off a bomb."

"That's terrorism! You're not a terrorist."

"So is going round shooting people terrorism. It's just a label. But I'm going to set the bomb off in the early morning when there's no-one there, and even if there's a security guard, I'll make sure they can get out before anything happens."

"You can do that?"

"Trust me. I'm making a statement this time, not looking for revenge."

HE PREPARED carefully. Fire, rather than an explosion, he reckoned, would hit the news more, and have a bigger visual impact on TV. His years in Afghanistan had taught him about the preparation and manufacture of improvised explosive and incendiary devices. More than anyone really should know, he thought to himself.

The materials were easy enough to obtain. Jeanine offered to get some of the less obvious components for the bomb. He accepted gladly, and sent her to stores in different parts of New York and across the river to New Jersey to buy them, making the trail as hard as possible to follow.

"You scare the shit out of me, Henry," Jeanine said to him, as he sat at the kitchen counter one evening with a toolkit, an electronic kitchen timer and a couple of spools of wire. "Do the Marines teach you this kind of thing?"

"Sort of, yeah. You get to know how the bad guys work, anyway."

"You're no bad guy," she told him. "You're on the right side."

"Wish I was as convinced as you are."

"Remember your sister and your kids. Hell, remember me and my kids."

He bent to the counter again, delicately soldering a connection. The fumes from the solder curled up and he looked at Jeanine. "I remember, don't worry." His voice was almost expressionless. "It's time that other people started to remember these things."

"How will they know?"

"You're going to send a message."

"Me?"

"Yes, you. But no-one's going to know it's you, don't worry. Use a public library over the river to set up a Hotmail mail account and send the message from there to this Hampton chick."

"Just her? Not the *Times* or anyone else?"

"Yep. I have a feeling about this one. She scares me, but I trust her at the same time."

"How do you mean?"

"She's smart – she knows why I've done all this, and I hope she never finds out that it's me who's been doing it. But at the same time, that article wasn't exactly on the side of the Wall Street guys."

"And if you make sure that no-one gets hurt when you do the agency, then she may well be on your side."

"That's what I'm hoping."

"Just as long as you don't expect her to come along and hold your hand while you're doing it. She's not going to cheer you on, you know."

THE FIRE-BOMBING OF THE RATINGS AGENCY, which gutted the building and shut down the business completely for three months, made the headlines. The night security guard, who had been the only person in the building, told reporters that he had heard a voice "out of nowhere", which told him to get out of the building. When asked to describe the voice, he said that it sounded like a woman's voice, with what might have been a Midwestern accent. "Not a New York kinda voice," he had said. He had been so spooked by the voice that he had run out of the front door. Thirty seconds after he had left the building, he reckoned, he heard a loud "whoomf" and turned to see flames exploding out of the first-floor front windows.

The fire spread rapidly, and the fire department had been unable to save anything of importance. The incident caused a bottleneck in processing the mortgage and other securities, as the other agencies lacked the expertise to deal with them.

No-one appeared to have seen or noted any-one or anything unusual at the time of the fire – three-thirty in the morning. There were few people around at that time of night, other than maintenance workers of various kinds, and there were no strange or suspicious persons reported in the area.

THE DAY AFTER the rating agency was firebombed, Kendra arrived at her desk to see Patricia sitting in the visitor's chair. She had obviously been crying.

"What's up, Pat?" she asked.

"Didn't you hear? Our offices burned to the ground. Arson. Someone hates us. Liz and Phil were right. They're coming for us."

"Oh my God." Despite the fact that she'd been expecting this, or something like it, Kendra was shocked. "Anyone hurt?"

"No, thank God. The watchman was warned by some sort of mysterious voice out of the darkness, he said. He got out of the building and the place went up less than a minute later."

"Any clues?

"Not that I've heard. No-one's said anything to you, then?

"I've only just got here, Pat." She logged into her computer and checked her email. "Wow. I reckon this has come to me because of the story I wrote. It's actually addressed to me by name. 'Rating bad mortgage as good is bad idea. Stop doing it.' Clear enough message?"

"Who's it from?"

"They didn't sign their name, that's for sure. Email address? xyzxyzxyz@hotmail.com. Cute. Could be anyone, setting up an account at the public library or something and sending it from there. No point trying to chase the sender through the addresses, I bet you." She printed off two copies of the message, and handed one to Patricia. "Pass it on to the police through Phil, would you?"

"Sure."

"It will probably won't do much good. You're still seeing Phil? Sorry, should have asked that first."

Patricia smiled shyly. "Yes, we seem to get on fine together. He's a good guy." She pursed her lips in thought. "Aren't you a little worried for yourself? I mean, this guy has your name and knows how to send you mail."

"Not really. I haven't thrown him out of his house or sold him a bad mortgage. I've just given the facts as I see them."

"Without mentioning me or my employers by name. Thank you for that, anyway. Anyway, I'll be off. Maybe I don't have an office to go to right now, but I wanted to just see how you were, and whether you knew any more than I'd seen on the TV."

"Phil would know more than me, I reckon."

"Guess he would at that. Take care of yourself, Kendra."

"And you, Pat. Use the time off. Take a break or something. Say hi to Phil."

Patricia had only been gone for ten minutes when the phone on Kendra's desk rang. It was her editor.

"Can you come into my office now? Drop whatever you're doing." There was something in the tone of his voice that she couldn't quite place.

Fearing the worst, she made her way to Mike's glassed-off corner office, carrying the printout of the email she had received. He had a worried look on his face.

"Do you think you're responsible for this?" he said, gesturing at the TV in the corner. The screen showed a talking heads shot of a Fire Department official, with the blackened remains of an office building in the background.

"Uh-huh. That's the rating agency?"

"It *was* the rating agency till the small hours of this morning, yes. Obviously I'm not asking if you set fire to the place, but in your opinion, did your article the other day – and it was a good article, don't get me wrong – inspire the lunatic who did this?"

"Not exactly. It might have made him act a little quicker than he was going to do otherwise, but I think he had the idea in his head already."

"Okay. Do you think you're next on his list? Because if you do, we'll take care of you. You can work in another office – overseas, if you like. We'll take care of you," he repeated.

"Not necessary," she answered. "You're the second person in fifteen minutes to ask me if I'm next on the list. The other was someone working in that agency," she gestured towards the TV.

"Want to stay on the story, then? We're not a tabloid or a crime sheet, but if you want to follow this up, you can. It might show the world that we care about more than five-year yields and aluminum futures. Good publicity for the whole group."

Kendra didn't hesitate. "Sure."

"We can hire security for you if you think you want it."

"Very sweet of you, Mike, but I don't think this guy, whoever he is, is going to be stopped by a couple of gorillas once he puts his mind to something."

"You make him sound scary."

"He *is* scary. This guy is driven, right? Something happened that has set him off on this killing spree. The connection is mortgages. Read this." She passed the printout of the email over to him. "Every single thing he's done has some connection somewhere to this whole steaming pile of dogshit that's the subprime mess. We all know here that it's all going to blow up in our faces real soon now. They've got to know that at the banks, and yet they carry on with this craziness." She stopped and caught her breath. "Sorry, you caught me on my pet subject just then."

Mike looked at her curiously. "You feel this, don't you? It's more than just an intellectual analysis, isn't it?"

"Yeah. There's folks being screwed left right and center across the country. And all their money is coming here." She jabbed her finger downwards. "New York. Specifically, Wall Street. It's not the way things are meant to be."

"It's not," Mike agreed. "But if you're so tied up with this thing, are you sure you should be covering it?"

"Damn it, Mike, that's exactly the reason why I should be covering it. This is more than an intellectual analysis, to use your words."

"Go ahead, then." He sighed. "But if you find me spiking some of your stories, because I think they're too emotional, don't act all surprised and hysterical."

"Since when have I ever been hysterical?"

He smiled. "Sure. Go ahead and dig up what you can. Take care of yourself, right? Come to me if you have any problems."

She returned to her desk, and started making notes.

"You know who else is involved in this?" Powers said to Jeanine, a few days after the rating agency. He'd been half-expecting a knock on the door of his apartment, or a heavy hand on the shoulder at work, following the message he'd sent to Hampton, but there was nothing.

"You're going to tell me, aren't you?"

"The Securities Exchange Commission – the SEC. They've been told about this shit, and they have the power to stop it happening. Instead of which, they just sit on their asses and let it all happen. Those motherfuckers deserve to die. They're meant to look after us, stop these Wall Street slimeballs from ripping us off, and they're not doing their jobs. They've let us down. That isn't what I fought for in Afghanistan, and what my buddies died for. They have to go." His voice rose.

"The SEC, that's Federal, right?"

He nodded.

"You can't do that, Henry."

"Do what?"

"Do whatever you're going to do. It's the Feds, Henry. They'll crucify you if they catch you."

"Then they'd better not catch me." He spoke brusquely, almost roughly.

"Are you going to tell me what you're going to do?" she asked.

"It's better if you don't know. In fact, I've been thinking that maybe you should go back to Brandi's place. Be with the kids. I'll meet up with you there when all this is over."

"And when will that be?"

"A week. Ten days."

"I want to be here with you."

He shrugged. "Please yourself."

That had been three days earlier. Since then, Jeanine had sulked, or at any rate, had kept her distance from him, especially at the times when he worked on the device he was building in the evenings.

"I should take that thing, whatever it is, away and throw it in the trash."

"You dare do that, and…" He said no more, but he could see that the unspoken words were more terrifying to her than any spoken threat he could have made.

He still put on his suit in the mornings, went to the bank, performed his duties there to perfection, but he could sense that something had changed inside him.. It didn't make his relationship with Jeanine any easier, and they almost stopped speaking to each other.

He'd finished his work on the bomb for the night. She'd been sitting on the couch, curled up like a nervous cat, not speaking to him, but she stretched as he stood up, and reached out her arms towards him.

He moved towards her, returned her embrace, and they stood for a minute, holding each other and not speaking.

"Henry?" she began, softly.

""Yes?"

"You're scaring me."

"I'm scaring myself," he confessed. "Up to now, I guess I was seeing myself as a surgeon. I was using a scalpel to take out the people who were fucking things up for people like you and Laroche. I was taking out cancers, if you like. Now it's different."

"I can see that. Can you tell me what you're thinking?"

"I want to, but I'm not sure I can do it. It's something like what I felt sometimes when I was fighting in Afghanistan. Like, you become less of a surgeon, and more of a bug exterminator."

"These are people you're talking about."

"I know, and I don't like myself for thinking this way. I can't help it, though. The adrenalin or whatever it was seems to take over. The people I'm up against seem to become less than human. Maybe that's something the Corps teaches you – how to see your enemies as less than real people. I read somewhere that one of the hardest jobs in military training is to get ordinary men to accept the idea of killing other people. That's why there's all that drill instructor bullshit. It's meant to knock the humanity out of you. And it worked on me. Those SEC bastards don't mean any more to me than a nest of cockroaches. And I know I shouldn't be thinking that way."

"You poor thing. That's no way to be." She stroked his cheek, and he flinched, but then relaxed. "You need help."

He laughed. "You're helping, believe me. I know what you mean, though. No-one's ever going to be able to help me with this one, though, are they? I'll go through with it, and then…"

"Then what? Are you going to be able to stop there? You say that these SEC guys aren't doing their job? What about Congress? What about the President?"

"I swore an oath when I joined the Marines." His face was set in a mask. "But… Oh God, Jeanine, you've just put into words something that I didn't dare think for myself. There's something bigger than me driving me on."

"I know there is," she answered him. "It's called the Devil."

He stared at her. "You're serious there?"

"Listen, Henry, you're a good man. I've seen that too often not to believe it. But what you're doing now, what you're thinking now, that's not good. That's not coming from you. It's coming from outside you. And you can call me dumb. You can call me a believer in fairy tales or something, but I believe there is a power of evil that lives outside us, and it's taken you over. And the long and the short of it is, Henry, that I can't live with you any more. So it's goodbye."

She slipped out of his arms, and moved to the door, where she picked up her bag that she'd packed while he'd been working at the kitchen counter. He stood there, stunned.

"Jeanine?" He appeared frozen.

"I may see you again, Henry. I hope I do. But I hope it will be the Henry I fell in love with, not the one I'm talking to now." Tears ran down her face. "I'm off to Wilmington. You know where you can find me." And with that, she was gone.

He couldn't even put into words what he was feeling. Loss, rage, anger, grief, all raced through his mind in bewildering succession. He turned to the bomb again, picked up the tools, and went back to work with a clinical intensity. Tomorrow night would be the night.

TWENTY-SIX: OCTOBER 2007

KENDRA HAD ONLY BEEN at her desk for thirty minutes when she got a call from reception. "Ms. Hampton, you have a visitor who says she wants to see you. She doesn't have an appointment."

"Does she say what it's about?"

"She says it's personal. And… I don't know how to put it politely, but she's not the usual type of visitor that we have here. She's passed security, though. No weapons."

Kendra sighed. "I'll come to reception and meet her."

Her visitor turned out to be a youngish black woman, who was certainly not dressed in the way that most visitors to FNS were turned out. If Kendra was being snobbish, she'd describe it as "Walmart chic". The woman spoke nicely enough, though, and introduced herself as "Jeanine".

"You have something to say to me?"

"Yeah. Can we go somewhere private?"

Kendra led the way to one of the small

conference rooms. "Before we start, tea? Coffee? Doughnut or something?"

"Coffee and doughnut sounds great." Jeanine smiled for the first time since Kendra had seen her.

Kendra picked up the phone, and the coffee and goodies were brought in.

"So, what do you have to say to me? And why me?"

"You wrote that article on the Wall Street murders, didn't you? That's why you."

"Yes." Kendra's heart was racing. This sounded as though it could possibly be the big scoop that every journalist dreams of.

"Do you promise me that you won't tell anyone what I'm about to tell you?"

"I don't know that I can make that promise. Journalists aren't doctors or priests, you know."

Jeanine picked up her coffee mug and took a sip before starting on her doughnut, which she ate slowly, in silence. Kendra waited. She knew that patience was needed sometimes to get the full story. This was one of those times. The last of the doughnut disappeared, and Jeanine drained the coffee.

"Thanks," She sat, looking at Kendra, seemingly coming to a decision. "What do you feel about the murders in Ohio?" she asked at length.

"What a question. I'll try to answer it as honestly as possible. It seems that the world is better off without that pastor and his friend. And that meth head and his girl don't seem to be a loss.

The two bankers? They don't seem to have been that popular. But someone killed them, and that's against the law. So I have to say that part of me applauds, and part of me thinks it was wrong for them to be killed that way."

"I see. What about those two traders or whatever they call themselves?"

"I knew one of them quite well and I kind of liked him as a person. It doesn't mean that I approved of what he was doing. I never knew the other guy. I can't say I'm happy about the idea of someone running round Wall Street knocking off traders."

"And the ratings people?"

"It seems that whoever's doing this made sure that no-one was going to get hurt. So good for them. And I know that the rating agencies are going to bring the economy crashing down, with the way that they're labeling the junk as good stuff. But again, what happened is against the law. How can I say it's a good thing?"

Jeanine sat there, looking at Kendra. "I've got to trust you, Ms. Hampton—"

"Kendra."

"Okay. I've got to trust you, because there's no-one else I can go to. He's a good man, Kendra."

"Who?" But she knew the answer.

"The man who's doing all this. Henry's a good man."

Bingo! Tall muscular black guy, military-looking, knows his way round Wall Street, could get close enough to Reichman and Sanfion to kill them before they knew anything was happening. Henry. The security guy at the Swiss bank. Kendra kept her face impassive. "Henry? Your husband?"

Jeanine shook her head. "A friend. A real good friend. At least, he was a good friend. Now he's not the person I first knew."

"How so?"

The words came out in a rush. "He's planning to blow up the SEC offices, I know, and he doesn't care who gets hurt when he does it."

"How do you expect me to keep quiet about that and not tell the police?"

"I was hoping that you could talk to him, and argue him out of it. Get him to go back home."

"To Ohio?" Kendra said this before she realized the implications.

"You know he's from Ohio?"

"I know who he is, Jeanine." Kendra said the words softly. "I've met him already and talked with him without knowing what he'd been up to."

"Oh." Jeanine slumped back in her chair. "Then you know what sort of person he is."

He might be a psychopath, Kendra thought to herself, but said nothing out loud. The sort that sits there quietly at a dinner party, with beautiful manners and exquisite smalltalk, and then goes out into the night to rape and murder. But then again, this woman obviously knew him quite well, And then once again, some of her friends were seemingly happily married to men who were total assholes, in her opinion. "He was certainly a charming man," she said. "And obviously a very strong character."

"He thinks you're smart," Jeanine said. "From meeting you that time, and from what you wrote. He might not listen to me, but he might listen to you."

"He's a Marine, isn't he? Since when do they listen to women?"

"He's not like that. I thought he was when I first met him. He's been really good with my kids, and good to me. I'm the one who's behaved like a bitch. The only reason I've walked out on him is because I want to save him. You've got to help me, and him." The tears started to flow.

"Tell me more," Kendra asked her. "When's he going to do this?"

"Soon, but I don't know when. Maybe tonight, or the night after. Within a week, anyway."

"And then what? Is he finished? Is that the end of it?"

More tears. "I don't know. I don't think so. Honestly, it wouldn't surprise me if he went off to DC and started all over again."

Shit, this was worse than she thought. "Are you sure about this? Look, just supposing I agree to help you with this, and I talk to him, and he doesn't agree to sort what he's doing? What's to stop him pulling out that big old Colt 45 of his and putting two bullets in my head, just to stop me talking to anyone else?"

"He wouldn't do that." Jeanine's tone was defiant. "Not if you gave your word that you wouldn't talk. I swear, he's a good man. It's just like this demon or something has got inside him, and he's not the man he should be."

The term for that is 'insanity', dear, Kendra thought, but didn't say. "Listen, Jeanine, this is going to be really tough for you, but if I can talk him out of it, can you get him to go for treatment or something if you think he needs it?"

"I'd do my best."

Kendra stood up and took Jeanine's hands in hers, looking directly into her eyes. "I'm going to help you. God knows why I am doing this, but I am. I'm in trouble if all this comes out, but it seems you're pretty sincere about him, and you're right, he didn't strike me as being a really bad man. So, you've got to help me. What's his name? He only called himself 'Henry' when I met him."

"Powers. Henry Powers. He was a major in the Marines. Major Henry Powers."

"I want you to stay here in this office all day. I'll be going out, but I'll make sure you can stay here. I'll make sure you're comfortable, have a TV to watch, send out for food, whatever. Okay? We're going to work together on this, and I want you close to me. First things, first, though." She picked up the phone and called the Swiss bank where Henry worked. "Kendra Hampton from FNS. Can you put me through to Henry Powers in security, please? Oh, really. Did he say when? Thank you." She put the phone down and stared at Jeanine. "He called in early and said he wasn't coming in. No reason."

"It's tonight, then," Jeanine said in a flat tone.

"If he's not at work, he'll be at the place you've been staying, right?"

"I guess."

"Let's go."

The cab deposited them outside the apartment building.

"Use your key, or ring the bell?" Kendra asked.

"Ring the bell. I don't want to scare him by walking in on him unannounced. God knows what he's thinking right now."

There was no answer, even after they'd pressed the bell several times.

"Then we use your key," Kendra told Jeanine. When they reached the apartment door, Kendra rang the bell and knocked loudly. There was no response. "In we go," said Kendra.

The apartment was empty. Not only was Henry gone, but there was no real sign that the place had ever been occupied, other than an empty coffee mug sitting by the kitchen sink, rinsed and upside down. There wasn't even anything in the trash cans. The bed had been stripped, and there were no clothes in the closets or the drawers.

"He's gone," said Jeanine. "He must have guessed I was going to tell someone about him, and he doesn't want to be found. So where would he have gone?"

"There's no way to tell," Kendra told her. "No way could anyone find him in this city. He could be anywhere. The only thing we can do is to tell the police that the SEC's going to be attacked some time soon, and to get them to put a police guard around the building."

"No!" Jeanine stamped her foot. "You're white, you don't know shit about the cops. You're white, you do something you're not supposed to, they slap you on the wrist and tell you not to do it again. You're black, you toss a gum wrapper on the street, and before you know it, bam! You're history. Some asshole cop's just used you for target practice. Listen, I know all about what he's been doing. I guess you could say I helped him. You call the cops, what's that going to do to me? I'm going to be fucked every which way from tomorrow if they get hold of me. They'll lock me up and throw away the key. I've got three kids." She started to cry.

"I hear you, Jeanine. Suppose you and I between us can't talk him out of it. What's he going to do?"

"I don't want to be anywhere near that fucking place when he is there, if there's going to be cops around."

"Then stay on the other end of the phone so he and I can talk to you if we need to."

"Sure, but I'm not going to tell you where I am."

"That's fine. Then I can tell the cops that, and we'll all be happy."

"Except the cops." Jeanine smiled.

TWENTY-SEVEN: OCTOBER 2007

KENDRA WAS BEGINNING TO FEEL that she was wasting her time. She'd been standing outside the entrance to the SEC offices for a few hours now. The security guards had picked her up, but she'd shown her press pass, and explained that she was waiting to "doorstop" one or two of the officials. Once she'd given the explanation, she was courteously invited to wait inside, but she declined with a smile, explaining that she preferred the fresh air after spending the first part of the day in an air-conditioned office.

"Can't say I blame you, lady," said the guard she was talking to. "That air-conditioning they have in the offices really does my sinuses in, know what I mean?" He was obviously in a mood to chat, and Kendra indulged him for a few minutes. He was pleasant enough, and Kendra flirted with him on a very mild and casual level.

"Who's the guy you want to talk to?" he asked her. "You wait over there and I'll give you a call when I see him."

"It's not a guy, actually. Jane de Souza, one of the executive directors, just come from DC on a visit," she told him.

He scratched his head. "Can't say I know her."

Hardly surprising, she thought to herself, considering she'd just made up the name and the title at random. "Never mind," she said. "I'll recognize her when I see her."

"Sure she's in today? I can call up and make sure."

"Don't worry yourself. I'd do this by phone usually, you know, but it's such a lovely day, I don't want to stay indoors. It's a great excuse for me to get out."

"Okay. I'm off at four. I'll tell the guy after me about you so he doesn't hassle you."

"That's very sweet of you. Thanks." She gave him a sweet smile and watched him melt at the knees.

It was now half-past five. She looked along the road, and Henry Powers appeared in the crowd.

His height and his bearing would have made him stand out in any group, but it was the grim determination that propelled him forward and showed on his face that marked him. She moved to stand in his way.

"Henry?"

For a moment, his face was blank, and then she saw his face change as he recognized her. "Ms. Hampton? What are you doing here?"

"Kendra, please. I was waiting for you." As if

they had been old friends, she slipped her arm through his, and walked beside him, past the SEC's entrance. She could feel something large, something lumpy and bulging, under the ratty old windcheater he was wearing. He looked very different from the sharply dressed dude she had met in the bank, and yet he hadn't changed that much.

"How did you know I was going to be here?" He made no move to disengage himself from her.

"Jeanine told me."

She was expecting an explosion, but it never came. Just a sigh. "I should have guessed. So you're going to call the cops?"

"Unless that's what you want, no."

This time he did break away from her, and stopped in her path, blocking her way, and looking down at her. "What the hell do you want, lady? Some kind of scoop interview with the Wall Street Killer?"

"Not that," she said. "Can I buy you a cup of coffee and we'll talk?"

He shrugged. "And if I say no? You'll call the cops?"

"Maybe. Maybe not. Depends on what you do."

"Okay." She took his arm once more, and steered them to a coffee shop where she ordered two cappuccinos from the barista. They found a table in the corner, well away from other patrons, and sat in silence. She felt him scrutinizing her face, while she avoided looking at him.

"What's under there?" she asked him in a low

voice, pointing to the windbreaker. "A bomb?"

He nodded.

"Big one?"

"Big enough."

"The problem with bombs is that you end up killing the wrong people."

"You're telling *me* that? I've been in Afghanistan, lady. I've seen HE fuck up more people that you would ever believe possible. People who didn't need to die. Tell you something, I don't care any more. What was it that guy said?"

"What guy?"

"Some dude a long, long time ago. They were attacking some city, and someone asked this guy who they should kill. See, there were good guys in that place and some bad guys. Who are you going to waste? That was the question. So you know what he said?"

"I remember something like that. 'Kill them all and God will sort them out afterwards.' That's you now?"

"Yeah." He sounded exhausted.

"And you'd planned to be one of the ones who died?"

"Yeah."

"Why in hell? You're a smart guy, you've got a woman that loves you—" He started. "—Give me some credit for recognizing love when I see it. Jeanine's seems like she's a pretty special sort of person and I don't know if you realize that."

"I'll tell you why." He leaned forward. Their faces were less than a foot apart, and she could feel his overheated breath as she spoke. "I'm turning into a monster. Something I'm not. Do you believe in the Devil?"

The question threw her off balance. "Er, not as such."

"Jeanine does. She told me last night that the Devil had taken me over. I reckon she might just be right at that."

"Go on." She sat there, not moving, even though something inside was telling her to get away, get away, before it was too late.

"You know how crappy the whole mortgage deal is. All these ABS, the fake credit ratings, the subprime shit. Well, it's not just the salesmen, not just the banks, not the Wall Street dudes, not even these SEC fuckers. It goes all the way to DC. To Congress and above. If I don't stop myself, I can see me and my friend," he opened the windbreaker slightly to reveal a Colt 45 in a shoulder holster, "going up to Washington to do some business together."

"So killing yourself along with a load of people who may be innocent is better?" He nodded. "I don't think so."

"Well fuck you!" he said, suddenly angry. "What the fuck do you know what happened?"

She resisted the urge to draw back, and simply replied, "Tell me."

So he did, tears in his eyes. By the end of the story, her eyes were also filled with tears, and she found she was holding his hand tightly, without any memory of how that had come to be.

He looked at her. "It all means something to you, then? You're crying."

"Of course it means something. It means that Jeanine's right. You're a decent guy underneath it all, and you know it."

"Thanks."

"Look, don't you think there's been enough death. These guys," she jerked a thumb over at the SEC, "deserve it, perhaps, but there may be a better way."

"Which is?"

"I'm a journalist, right? I'm pretty good at it, you know. If I wrote about your story, people would read about it. They'd know about what your sister went through. What Jeanine went through. All the crap that the banks have pulled."

"You can remember all that I've told you?"

"I knew a lot of it already, remember. But yeah, I can remember it. I'm a journalist, remember. And even if I get some of the details wrong, it makes it harder to identify you, doesn't it?"

"You'd change the names, of course?"

"Of course. Names, places, everything. Change everything enough that you can't be identified. Might take you out of the Marines and put you in the Army."

He grinned. "Trying to insult me, are you?" The smile faded. "You reckon people would read it?"

"It might be a book. With TV appearances by me. Yeah, it will get read, believe me. Mind you, I'd try and change my name and move to a different part of the country, if I were you. Seattle's nice, I hear, if you don't mind the rain."

"And then?"

"And then you've made your point. I don't believe you pulled all this crap simply for revenge, did you? You were trying to make people realize what was going on in this country, I guess."

"Guess that was at least part of it, yeah."

"Trouble is, that your way of getting attention was the way the Marines taught you to get people's attention. With a gun."

"Smart analysis. You might just be right at that."

"And at some point, Jeanine's right. The Devil walked in. My way of getting attention is better. With luck, someone's going to wake up and ask what's going on, and the people responsible are going to find themselves in trouble. Listen, you saw the way that those Wall Street guys lived, didn't you?"

"Yeah."

"What hurts them more? A couple of bullets to the head, or losing everything and spending five years in prison?"

"I see what you're saying. Look, you've got to let me think about this, right?"

"Sure."

He seemed to be thinking aloud as he spoke in a low voice, more to himself than her, it appeared.

"Would I be happy if I saw the law take care of all of this? Sure I would. Revenge is a crazy game, anyway. Sure, some of this was dumb revenge, but you've got to believe that the shit I pulled here in this city was more than that."

"A cry for help?"

"If you want to put it that way, yes. Not a cry for someone to help me, but a cry for someone to help America. We've taken the wrong turnings and it's time for someone to get us back on the right path. I thought maybe I could be that person."

"Maybe on your own, you can't do that. Maybe what you've done and me writing about it might make things change a bit. Help get things back on track. Get people thinking."

"You can't promise that's going to happen, though, can you?"

"I can promise to do my best to make sure it does. You've done your part. Let me do mine."

He appeared to consider it for all of three seconds. "Done deal. You're right. Thank you."

"Come with me. Let's get rid of that old Devil, shall we?" She dragged him to his feet and led him to the yacht harbor, deserted now. "See that there," she said, pointing to the water. "Your friend under your jacket goes for a little swim there. No-one's ever going to find him down there, and there's no way the ballistics will ever point to you. As long as you got that gun, you can be fingered."

He paused, and then reached under the windbreaker. "You know, I've been wanting to do this for a long time," he said, taking the gun and flinging it into the water in a wide arc. "Thanks."

"What about… the other?" she asked.

"Wait a moment," he said, fumbling with

something that appeared to be encircling his waist, and coming up with a small battery, which followed the gun into the water. "Now it's safe." A little more fumbling, and he had a clumsy contraption in his hands that looked like a workman's tool belt. "Thank you for talking me out of this." There was a splash as it sank, leaving a trail of bubbles that rose to the surface. "That was actually a pretty neat piece of handiwork," he said, with a smile she hoped was ironic. "The Taliban would have been proud of me."

"And that's it? There's nothing else?"

"Nothing. Jesus, Kendra. I don't know what to say. Thanks."

"Call Jeanine. Now. She's waiting to hear from you."

He pulled out his cellphone, and she retired to a discreet distance, watching as he spoke, a smile of pure delight spreading over his face as he talked. He hung up, and walked over to her.

"Jeanine says to give you a kiss from her." He kissed her. "And here's one from me." He repeated the kiss. "We're meeting at La Guardia, and flying off to a secret undisclosed location, as they like to say. Her kids will be joining us later. You won't see us or hear from us again. But we'll keep an eye open for you."

"Thanks. God knows if we're all doing the right thing here, Henry, but I'm pretty sure we are."

"I know we are. Not just for me, but for Jeanine and the kids. Thank you, Kendra." He put his arms around her and hugged her tight.

"Ouf. Now let me go, and go and catch your plane."

"Sure thing. You in some sort of hurry to get rid of me?" He hailed a cab, and got in. "Bye," he called through the cab window.

"Bye."

Sure I'm in a hurry, she said to herself. I've got a book to write. A book that tells the story of a decent man, driven to desperate measures by a system and a morality that nearly destroyed his life.

BEVERLY THOMAS

IN 2007, while most in the United States were riding high on a perceived good economy, supplementing their incomes by refinancing their homes. That is, they used the equity in their homes to cash out large sums of cash. It worked quite well for a while. Then they were faced with repaying those loans.

During this time, I was attending a program in Real Estate Development at the University of Southern California Lusk Center for Real Estate. I watched in astonishment as Southern California properties that two years previously sold for $250,000, were now selling for $1,000,000. There was a veritable feeding frenzy in the real estate industry, where investors were snapping up properties, mortgage brokers were fitting anyone who had a job with a mortgage for the dream homes the real estate agents were aggressively selling. Worse, predatory lenders were stalking minority home owners with high-interest refinanced mortgages. It amazed me that nobody, including my classmates, seemed to see what was patently obvious to me: this was an abnormal real estate and banking environment fueled by derivative trading and illusory mortgage and real estate deals. Nothing was real, and it would all fail. Soon. I was regrettably prescient.

Unfortunately, the real estate bubble burst, and as Henry Powers discovered, unprincipled characters had managed to nearly bring the entire global economy to its knees.

What can people do if they find themselves in Jeanine's situation?

1. Read all of your mail. There is information in there that you can use to save your home. Setup a file, collect all correspondence in it. Keep a diary of all contact with anyone involved in your situation. Collect all of your financial information in a file, including wage, pension and Social Security check stubs, bank, mortgage, insurance and tax statements, and anything else pertaining to your finances. Keep them up to date. I cannot stress how vital this is.

2. Consult counselors. The U.S. Government provides free assistance. Immediately set up an appointment with the U.S. Government Department of Housing and

Urban Development(HUD)in your area.
They have solutions, including special pro-
grams to assist homeowners in distress.
http://portal.hud.gov/hudportal/
HUD?src=/topics/avoiding_foreclosure

3. The National Housing Institute provides
resources designed to avoid foreclosures
and how to obtain mortgage modifications. There is also information pertaining
to the foreclosure process.
http://www.nhi.org/resources/
foreclosure/

4. Contact neighborhood assistance agencies
such as:
Neighborhood Assistance Corporation of
America
https://www.naca.com/naca/index.aspx
Freddie Mac
http://www.freddiemac.com/singlefam-
ily/service/hfa_relief.html

5. Check your local and state government
agencies.

6. Check your local, state, and feder-
al officials, such as City and County
Council members, or U.S. Congress
Representatives.

7. Check your local colleges and universities
for free and lowcost resources.

8. My most productive resource has been the
bank holding the mortgage. I wrote letters to the president and CEO. I received
immediate responses and the modification

request received priority processing. It pays to speak up. Attend the public conferences that the bank hosts. Often they have all of their representatives on-site to process your modification request. One-on-one requests are invaluable. They work. It puts a face on the request.

9. Use on-line searches for available resources. Google is your friend here.

10. Keep in mind that the foreclosure process can take years to complete, especially if you fight back. You will not have to move from your home during this time. So keep on fighting!

11. Keep your spirits up, take care of your health. Never give up. And until there is absolutely no other resource or option available, do not move out of your home! Once you move, your options end.

If you have further questions, you can reach me at:

The National Association of University Women, Southwest Section (facesouthwest@nauw1910-sw.org).

We may have further advice based on our experience with foreclosures and modifications.

Beverly L. Thomas

FROM THE AUTHOR & PUBLISHER

Of course we hope this book will make it to the top of the NYT best-seller lists, but, to be honest, the chances of that happening are remote, so we have to rely on people like you to spread the word.

We hope you enjoyed this book. Please let us and others know by sharing your thoughts with others. One of the best ways of doing this is through writing a brief review and posting it on Amazon, Barnes & Noble, or another book-related site, such as Goodreads. And even if you didn't like the book, it's always interesting for us to know why you didn't like it.

Thank you – we look forward to seeing your comments.

Hugh Ashton moved from the UK to Japan in 1988, where he lived for 28 years, mostly in the historic town of Kamakura, a little to the south of Yokohama, with his wife, Yoshiko.

He is best known for his Sherlock Holmes stories, which have been hailed as some of the most authentic pastiches on the market, and have received favourable reviews from Sherlockians and non-Sherlockians alike.

He currently lives in the Midlands cathedral city of Lichfield, where he and Yoshiko moved in 2016.

More about Hugh Ashton and his books may be found at:

HughAshtonBooks.com

and he may be contacted at:

Author@HughAshtonBooks.com

ALSO BY HUGH ASHTON:

Beneath Gray Skies
Red Wheels Turning
At the Sharpe End
Tales of Old Japanese
The Untime
The Untime Revisited
Leo's Luck
Angels Unawares
The Persian Dagger

SHERLOCK HOLMES TITLES:

Tales from the Deed Box of John H. Watson M.D.
More from the Deed Box of John H. Watson M.D.
Secrets from the Deed Box of John H. Watson M.D.
The Darlington Substitution
The Trepoff Murder
The Deed Box of John H. Watson M.D.
Notes from the Dispatch-Box of John H. Watson M.D.
Further Notes from the Dispatch-Box of John H. Watson M.D.
The Death of Cardinal Tosca
Without My Boswell
The Last Notes from the Dispatch-Box of John H. Watson M.D.
1894
Notes on Some Singular Cases of Mr. Sherlock Holmes
The Adventure of Vanaprastha

FOR CHILDREN

(WITH ILLUSTRATIONS BY ANDY BOERGER):

Sherlock Ferret and the Missing Necklace
Sherlock Ferret and the Multiplying Masterpieces
Sherlock Ferret and the Poisoned Pond
Sherlock Ferret and the Phantom Photographer
The Adventures of Sherlock Ferret

www.ingramcontent.com/pod-product-compliance
Lightning Source LLC
Chambersburg PA
CBHW031007190726
48286CB00003BA/723